For Josiah

HAETAE A novel written by Joe MENOSKY

Publishing fitbook
Publisher Seongwon JEONG
Copy editor Scott PEARSON
Design Junghwan MAENG
Illustration KUSH (@kushgraphic)
Marketing Kiljeong JEONG, Sonya KIM(김소영), Soyool JIN

Printed in the Republic of Korea
First Published in Feb. 10, 2024 (Seollal : Korean New Year's Day)

ISBN 979-11-085465 2 4

48, Jandari-ro, Mapo-gu, Seoul, Republic of Korea (04038)
Tel. 070-7856-0100 Fax. 0504-096-0078
E-Mail fitbookcom@naver.com
Instagram @fitbook_story
Blog blog.naver.com/fitbook_ing

Copyright © 2024 by Joe MENOSKY

All rights reserved. This book or any portion thereof may not be reproduced or used in any manner whatsoever without the written permission of the copyright owner except for the use of brief quotations in a book review.

All motif types referenced throughout this novel are from Motif-Index of Folk-Literature: A Classification of Narrative Elements in Folktales, Ballads, Myths, Fables, Mediaeval Romances, Exempla, Fabliaux, Jest-Books, and Local Legends by Stith Thompson, revised and enlarged edition, Indiana University Press, Bloomington, Indiana, 1955–1958.

HAETAE

Joe MENOSKY

HAETAE

Author's note

1. Beginning

2. Middle

3. Ending

Recommendation

　제가 아주 어렸을 때, 학교 선생님 자격으로 전 세계를 여행하던 이모가 계셨어요. 이모는 방문하는 나라마다 현지 전통 스타일로 만든 어린이용 모자를 보내주셨어요. 그래서 어린 시절에 저는 뉴욕이나 로스앤젤레스를 알기도 전에 한국을 비롯한 6개의 나라를 알게 되었습니다. '갓'을 쓰고 돌아다니는 아이는 아마도 우리 동네에서 저 밖에 없었을 겁니다.

　저는 오리지널 스타트렉 시리즈가 방영되기도 전에 사랑에 빠졌습니다. 곧 방영될 새 TV 프로그램의 광고가 라디오를 통해 흘러나오며 '스타트렉'이라는 제목을 듣자마자 "바로 이거야!"라고 외쳤답니다. 지금까지 그 어떤 것도 저의 상상력에 그렇게 큰 영향을 미치지는 못했죠. 현대의 신화 그 자체인 스타트렉은 제가 평생을 추구하게 될 신화와 민속에 거대한 영감이 되었습니다.

　몇 년 동안 한국의 전래동화 모음집도 읽었어요. 그러던 중 2007년에 한국TV드라마 〈태왕사신기〉를 보고 원천소스라고 생각되는 삼국유사까지 죽 읽었죠. 그리고 몇 년 후에 첫 소설을 구상하기 위해 한국을 처음 방문했을 때는 이미 제 마음에 한국의 신화와 민속이 자리 잡고 있었습니다.

Author's note

When I was very young, I had an aunt who travelled the world working as a schoolteacher. From each country she visited she would send me a child's hat fashioned in the local, traditional style. As a result, I was made aware of Korea and half a dozen other nations before I had heard of New York or Los Angeles. Certainly, I was the only kid in my neighborhood running around with a gat on his head.

I fell in love with the original Star Trek series before it even premiered. An advertisement for the upcoming new show came over the radio, and when they announced the title—Star Trek—I shouted "This is it!" Nothing else I had read or seen would have such an impact on my imagination. As a modern mythos itself, Star Trek also inspired my lifelong pursuit of mythology and folklore.

That included, down the years, collections of Korean folk tales. Then, in 2007, I saw Story of the First King's Four Gods and went on to read its source material, Samguk yusa.

So a few years later, when I visited Korea for the first time researching my first novel, I already had Korean mythology and folklore in the back of my mind. In Seoul,

서울 어디를 가든 해태와 마주치곤 했습니다. 경복궁 앞의 기념비적인 해태 한 쌍뿐만 아니라 정부청사, 은행 사무실 옆, 오피스텔 옆, 공항 내부, 남산 꼭대기, 심지어 택시에서도 만날 수 있었죠. 서울시의 상징 캐릭터인 '해치'는 해태를 인간의 모습으로 형상화한 것이기도 하죠. 흔하게 볼 수 있었지만 해태는 너무나 매력적이었고, 저는 그 매력에 푹 빠졌습니다. 이렇게 다양한 방식으로 표현되어 널리 퍼져있음에도 불구하고 해태는 본연의 매력을 잃지 않았고, 저는 그 매력에 푹 빠졌습니다.

세종대왕 이야기의 초고를 완성한 날, 바로 해태 이야기를 시작했을 정도였죠.

저는 이 이야기가 판타지이자 공상과학이라고 생각합니다. 이야기의 주인공인 신과 도깨비는 어떤 공간에 사는 존재입니다. 프랑스의 학자 앙리 코빈이 말한 상상의 세계에서 살아가는 존재들이죠. 코빈은 인간의 상상력에 의해 만들어진 세계이지만 동시에 종교적 신비주의를 통해 접근할 수 있는 독립적으로 존재하는 영역이라고 주장한 바 있습니다.

저는 코빈의 상상 세계에 등장하는 천사 같은 존재들 외에도 사람들까지 그곳에 밀어 넣으면 어떨까 생각했습니다. 산타클로스까지 포함해서요.

물질과 생각의 중간에 있는 이 상상의 공간에 신화나 민담, 전설 속에 등장하는 모든 것들이 '존재'합니다. 저는 그런 존재들이 일시적으로 그들의 본거지를 떠나 어떻게 우리에게 오게 할 수 있을까 고민했습니다. 저는 한국의 무속신앙에서 해답을 찾았습니다.

one is confronted by haetae—the very literal face of Korean mythology and folklore—at every turn. Not just the monumental pair in front of Gyeongbok Palace. But flanking government buildings and bank offices, next to officetels and inside the airports, on top of Namsan Mountain and adorning the doors of taxis. It is, in fact, the official mascot of the city of Seoul, represented as an anthropomorphized Haetae referred to as "Haechi" Despite this ubiquity and the multitude of ways in which it is depicted, the creature never loses its charm—and I was most definitely charmed. The same day I finished the first draft of a King Sejong the Great story, I started my first pass at a story about the haetae.

I consider this novel to be science fiction as much as fantasy. Despite the gods and the goblins, all such monstrous creatures dwell in an actual—or at least philosophically proposed—place: the Imaginal World of French scholar Henry Corbin. This theologically speculated location, Corbin claimed, is accessed by way of religious mysticism, a realm that is both created by the human imagination and simultaneously exists independently of it. But in addition to the angelic beings of Corbin's Imaginal World, I proposed we shove everybody in there: Santa Claus included. All figures of mythology and folktale and legend therefore "exist" in this space halfway between matter and thought.

Then it's a question of how to get such entities to temporarily leave their home base and pay a visit to ours.

전혀 다른 다른 두 개의 신화가 오늘의 서울이라는 같은 장소, 같은 전장에서 만났을 때 어떤 일이 벌어질지 보고 싶었습니다.

전설적 존재인 '해태'에 대해 그동안 많은 스토리를 접하기 어려웠기 때문에 조각상을 보는 것만으로도 매우 흥미로웠습니다. 해태는 마치 네발로 서 있는 요새처럼 보입니다. 머리를 살펴보면 보면 괴물처럼 보일 수 있는 해태를 동글동글한 모양과 커다란 얼굴로 표현해 마치 강아지처럼 보이게도 합니다. 해태는 위협적이면서도 귀여운 매력을 동시에 지닌 존재죠. 특유의 미소를 한번 생각해 보세요. 반은 으르렁거리면서도 반은 씩 웃는 듯한 표정, 특유의 큰 이빨도 위험하면서도 코믹한 느낌을 받습니다. 우스꽝스러우면서도 예측할 수 없는 존재죠.

'던전 앤 드래곤'에도 해태가 등장합니다. 게임 속에서 해태는 '법의 혼돈'에 해당하는 캐릭터인데 법과 혼돈은 서로 허용할 수 없는 조합입니다. 모든 신화 속의 존재를 본질적으로 정의내리기 불가능하다지만, 해태는 그 자체가 모순인 존재이기에 더욱 특별한 존재라고 할 수 있습니다.

실제 서울 한복판에서 해태가 사람들과 함께 숨 쉬며 돌아다닌다고 상상한 것처럼, 이 책을 읽는 모든 분들도 저와 같은 상상을 한번 해보시기를 바랍니다.

조 메노스키

For that, I proposed a version of Korean shamanism as the conduit. I wanted to see what would happen if two very different mythologies were thrown together in the same location or on the same battlefield—Seoul, today.

As there is not a large corpus of tales about this legendary figure, it was the statuary alone that got me intrigued. Haetae is a fortress on four legs. But its rounded shape and oversized facial features lend a puppylike aspect to what might be otherwise only monstrous. Instead, it is a beast that manages to be both intimidating and cute.

Consider the signature smile. Halfway between a snarl and a grin, the typically overlarge teeth evoke the sense of being simultaneously comical and dangerous. Or at the same time principled and a loose cannon. As a Dungeons & Dragons characterization alignment, haetae would be "Lawful Chaotic"—which is an unallowable combination. So if all mythological beings are by definition impossible, haetae is an IMPOSSIBLE impossible being, composed of unresolvable contradictions and therefore unique. It is my hope the reader might see in these pages even a glimpse of the same creation of the collective Korean imagination that I encountered in its natural habitat.

Joe Menosky

1. Beginning

Motif Types

B19.10. Mythical tiger.

A1414. Origin of fire.

L111.4.4. Mistreated orphan hero.

S31. Cruel stepmother.

F1. Journey to otherworld as dream or vision.

D1133. Magic house.

D1138. Magic tent.

J952.1. Presumptuous wolf among lions.

D494. Transformation: person to monster.

H1558. Tests of friendship.

"Long, long ago...

'Back when tigers smoked pipes,' as we say in Korea, 'Once upon a time,' as they tell it in English, or in Hungarian, 'Long ago, across seven countries, through the glass mountains, where the curly-tailed pig roots around'—fire was discovered.

A primordial-type deity named Miruk was annoyed about eating his rice raw for like a billion years. He knew he needed fire, but he didn't know how to make it. After beating up a few animals trying to get the secret out of them and having no luck at all, he cornered a mouse and the mouse spilled the beans. As it were. Mouse leapt off a piece of quartz trying to get away, which tumbled and struck against an iron meteorite embedded in the ground. Sparks flew! And Miruk figured out the rest.

That's how it happened in old Korea.

On the Caroline Islands of the West Pacific Ocean, a little bird flew down to the Earth with a burning branch in its beak, which is kind of sweet. Most of the time, though, somebody steals it.

In ancient Greece, for example, a demigod named Prometheus stole fire either from Zeus or from the workshop of Vulcan, depending on who is telling the tale, and gave it to the local humans, who like Miruk over in Korea, were also eating stuff raw up until then—just not rice. Barley or whatever.

Don't forget Prometheus. He'll be making a dramatic appearance a bit later.

And if you're wondering why I, Windy Lee, Seoulite, uneducated by choice, burdened by more han than is reasonable for a twenty-five-year-old, know about all these folktales, legends and myths: I had to learn. A matter of self-preservation."

The pair of stone statues of Haetae—mythological, fire-eating creatures on display in front of the main gates to Gyeongbokgung Palace—appeared to be on guard for the night shift.

The monstrous beasts were depicted with a muscular, thick body covered in scales, like a cross between a lion and a rhino, its signature and identifying element the subtle, Cheshire Cat-like smile always on its face, which made it simultaneously intimidating and endearing.

" 'Once upon a time' in Seoul—actually not: the time was exactly 8:29 p.m., April 7, 1998. And as for tigers, well, tigers <u>still</u> smoked. In a manner of speaking."

An old tiger walked slowly down the corridor of a modest, ten-story officetel in Seochon, past the residential doors on either side.

"An ancient Roman said 'Myths are things that never happened but always are.'"

As the tiger moved, the carpet from where it lifted its paws emanated smoke.

"Which means tigers are always smoking..."

The huge cat suddenly leapt toward the large window at the end of the corridor—and vanished in midair.

Sirens interrupted the silence of the palace grounds as the fire trucks screamed past.

The red-yellow from their flashing emergency lights bounced off the stone eyes of the Haetae, illuminating them with an unnatural golden glow: as if awakening something inside.

A one-year-old girl was sitting on the floor in the middle of a room filling with smoke.

"I looked adorable, I'm pretty sure, despite the fumes in my eyes that had already killed my mom."

Her mother was in the next room, slumped across a sofa, unconscious, overcome by the smoke.

"My dad was conveniently at the apartment across town he had with his other wife as if he was some

kind of Joseon dynasty princeling and so survived the blaze to be browbeaten by his half-orphaned daughter over the next twenty-four years for that unforgivable betrayal—but we'll get to that part soon enough."

Tendrils of smoke like vipers slid into the room, surrounding the baby. She gave a little cough.

"Little Me was moments away from being consumed by fire. And as you might have guessed, since I'm telling you this tale right now, that's not how it transpired. I won this round."

The apartment building had become a raging blaze by the time the fire trucks arrived. The firefighters shouted commands at each other and rushed into the building like it was a military assault.

An older man, Firefighter Heo, was the last inside, trailing the others and his own partner. He always hung back, as a rule, when entering a burning building. Not because he was afraid of what was inside, though he was. But because he always had an intuition about where to find the most helpless human being in a fire. Nobody ever berated him for this tardiness, because they knew it was true. It had happened too often to say otherwise. The firefighters split up into pairs, heading right, left, and up the stairs of the burning building.

An explosion from one of the upper floors suddenly blasted out the windows. Onlookers screamed.

The captain shouted into his radio for the benefit of his team inside, "Tenth floor is gone!"

Firefighter Heo was at the top of a stairway when he heard the captain's voice in his helmet radio order everyone to pull back—and the immediate response from his squad mates.

"Team 101! Survivors on nine, eight, and seven!"

"All teams assist!" replied the captain, without hesitation.

"Team 107-2! Copy that!" responded Heo, as he motioned to his partner, who nodded in confirmation and rushed back down the stairs. Just as the older man turned to join him, a movement caught his eye: a baby girl had crawled onto the landing above.

The older man was stunned. He shouted into his radio. "A survivor! Survivor on floor ten…"

Outside, watching the blaze get the upper hand, the captain heard the words that someone in his position never wants to hear.

"…a baby!"

"107-1!" shouted the captain without hesitation. "Get back up there!"

Heo's partner, who had just left him to assist downstairs, reversed direction to go right back up again. "Copy that!"

Whoosh! A blast of fire suddenly burned away the stairs above him. He fell backward, tumbling down the stairwell, catching hold of the handrail in just enough time to stop himself from breaking his neck. "Stairway's gone!" he shouted into his radio. "I can't do it!"

Firefighter Heo heard the blast below him, rushed up the remaining stairs, grabbed the baby and—barely ahead of the flames that now seemed to be following him—hauled the tiny girl out of the stairwell and into the nearest corridor.

At his command position outside, the captain quickly examined a blueprint of the apartment building, one goal overwriting everything else in his mind: save the child. "Teams 102 and 104! Access floor ten by the utility elevator shaft in the northeast corner!"

Inside the building one pair of firefighters rushed along an unburned corridor, responding to the team leader. "104 copy! 104 copy!"

Another pair guided a lone survivor to an open window and the rescue ladder extending to meet them from below.

One of them responded. "103 copy that!"

His partner indicated the survivor. "I got this!"

The other man immediately turned and ran back the way they had come to assist with the infant on floor ten.

Firefighter Heo had the baby in his arms as he rushed

along an unburned but smoky corridor. "I've got her! Heading to the northeast utility shaft now—"

He turned a corner: a wall of flames was in front of him, burning its way along the corridor. There was no way he could possibly go through it. Even by himself. Let alone with a fragile infant in his arms.

"Ah, hell," he said aloud, forgetting in the moment it would be radioed to everybody on the team.

His captain's voice instantly responded, "What? 107-2 report!"

Heo heard a boom behind him. He turned to see that the stairway he had just come up was now entirely aflame. The sound it made was a low, eerie crackle.

As if the fire was laughing at him.

"Report!"

"Captain..." said Firefighter Heo, in a calm voice, "there's nowhere for us to go."

The captain heard this just as the northeast corner of the building blew out along its windows floor by floor, going upward like a roman candle.

"Captain!" radioed another voice from the building, as the three firefighters trying to go to Heo's assistance watched the same series of explosions on the inside. "The utility shaft is gone!"

The captain gave the blueprint one more look and crossed off with his pen the stairway and the utility elevator shaft from what was left of the ways onto the tenth floor.

"All access points are blocked," he radioed to his team.

The three men confronted by the blown utility shaft heard a terrifying wrenching of metal: a burning elevator dropped right past them. They pulled back to avoid the heat as it passed, finally smashing far below with another eruption of flames. As if to underscore the captain's declaration: no access to floor ten.

Firefighter Heo and the tiny girl in his arms indeed had nowhere to go.

The fire moved slowly, like a predator approaching its prey. Heo kept his radio channel open and sending. "She's not even crying."

The captain, Heo's team partner, and the three who could not reach him all waited with absolute dread for the end of this horrible situation: terrible deaths they could no longer even attempt to prevent.

Heo pulled the child to his chest, as if to shield her as long as possible from the approaching flames. "It's okay, Little Baby… you're gonna be okay…" He closed his eyes and prayed for this tiny soul who would never know the world.

The baby's eyes were still open. And again, amazingly, she did not cry or struggle. But seemed to be... *waiting.*

And then the fire, which had been creeping as though hunting made its leap: with a terrifying roar, the flames surged forward for the kill.

The baby's pupils suddenly expanded to fill her eyes, and Heo heard the sound of rushing wind, as strong as a tornado. The enormous black mirror of the child's eyes reflected an image of flames tearing past at high speed, and the roaring sound of the fire became a kind of shrieking.

As if the fire itself was afraid.

Heo opened his eyes. Their surroundings were charred and destroyed, but the flames were gone. In disbelief, he looked down at the baby in his arms. She was unharmed.

Suddenly, she gave little burp.

And a tiny tendril of smoke slipped out of her mouth.

"After that, I started sleepwalking. Even before I learned to walk."

Windy Lee, four years later, wandered with eyes half-closed into the small kitchen of a modest apartment in the Yaksu neighborhood of Seoul. She bumped into a table and knocked a pan onto the floor with a clatter. The sound didn't even wake her up. Neither did the shouts of annoyance from the bedroom nearby. Her father and stepmother appeared at the door to the kitchen a few moments later, knowing full well what had happened, as this was a regular occurrence. A small dog barked angrily at young Windy, as a kind of extension of its owner, Windy's stepmother. The woman gave the girl a swat that woke her up. Windy didn't cry, just stared at them.

"I hate when she does that," said her stepmother, regarding Windy's concentrated gaze."

"That's my father and that's my father's other wife. And that's P'atjwi doing all the barking. I'm guessing ever since Cinderella, stepmothers have gotten a bad rap worldwide. But in her case, it was deserved. She took to locking me in the pantry, and that led to some easily foreseeable accidents."

Windy was asleep on a thin pad on the floor of the pantry, surrounded by shelves lined with bags of rice and bottles of sesame oil and jars of pepper paste. She rose to her feet, asleep, eyes glassy, and tried to shake open the door: it just rattled. Another shake. Another rattle. Then there was a tinkling sound and a puddle formed on the floor around her feet.

The next morning, young Windy stepped out of the apartment building. Shockingly, she had been stripped naked by her stepmother, a makeshift "dunce cap" had been strapped to her head, and a small wooden bowl put into her hands.

The woman's voice shouted from inside the house. "Go on!"

With an unhappy look in her eyes, Windy started walking, victim of a method of ritual familial humiliation that had gone out of style decades before. A few minutes later, Windy stepped inside the local general store, holding out the bowl. The owner was appalled. An old woman customer who had been chatting with him just stared.

"Don't come in here like that!" he shouted at Windy. "You tell that woman if she does this to you again, I'm calling the police! What does she think this is? The nineteenth century?"

But the little girl just held up the bowl.

"Go home!" he insisted.

Windy didn't budge.

"Oh, for God's sake," said the old woman, "give the poor child some salt."

The owner scowled, found an open bag of salt and poured some out into Windy's bowl. Then the girl turned and headed back out the door.

"She'll go to jail next time!" the owner shouted after her. "It's abuse! Tell her I said so! Abuse!"

"That sort of thing went on for a few more years.

Then, when I was ten..."

Five years later, Windy at ten was playing by herself on the floor of the apartment, watching as her stepmother went by with an armful of what looked like papers. The woman stepped onto the small balcony, where she already had a small BBQ brazier fired up. She shoved the papers—documents and photos—into the flames.

Windy glanced down at something the woman had dropped as she passed: a photo of the infant Windy and her mother when she was alive.

"...She gathered up all of my father's photos and mementoes of my mom and baby me to burn them—but I caught her."

Windy's eyes went wide as she realized what her stepmother was doing.

"And I won Round Two against the flames."

Her eyes suddenly got even wider: pupils filling the whites of the eyes as they had done when she was moments away from being consumed by fire as a baby.

On the balcony, a sudden rush of violent wind, as if from a super vacuum inside the apartment, snuffed out the brazier fire and pulled the load of photos and papers right from the woman's arms and whisked it into the apartment. Even the tiny dog was lifted momentarily off its feet and swept inside, yelping in confusion.

"Which freaked her out so severely that she steered clear of me for what has so far been the rest of my life."

Windy's eyes were back to normal in a few moments—leaving her dazed and unaware of what had just happened—as the old photos of her mother and her own childhood, her early crayon drawings, and other mementoes drifted through the air and spiraled down around her, picturesquely singed but unharmed by the flames. Her stepmother stood in the balcony and watched, a look of absolute terror on her face. The dog just whimpered in a corner.

"Turns out I can eat fire. If 'eat' is the right word. Snuff out, extinguish, obliterate, annihilate, also work. And not me exactly: but the Haetae inside of me."

Windy Lee, in her midtwenties, was seated in a city bus, a college backpack on her lap, idly watching the public TV monitor displaying the local weather report for the bus riders.

"Two major urban blazes in the last three months sent enough smoke and dust into the atmosphere to cause rain," announced the weathercaster, standing in front of satellite footage of two huge fires, one in the Gangnam neighborhood of Seoul, the other near Hongik University north of the river Han. "Twice as much as last year over the same time period. That includes today: with a sixty percent change of precipitation from now until 7 p.m."

Windy ate from a bag of chips that had a Haetae image emblazoned on the package as the brand's logo.

"Haetae are mythical Korean monsters, famous for protecting Seoul from being destroyed by fire. There are images of them everywhere around town. Looking both cute and scary which is a good trick."

Windy had a smock on for a class in ceramics at the junior college she was attending. She watched and waited as the instructor tried to fire up the kiln. "I don't know why I can't seem to keep the kiln lit when you are around, Miss Lee."

Windy was just as baffled.

"And it's not exactly inside of me: more like I'm a host or a channel like a natural mudang shamaness who brings the monster temporarily into this world. A creature out of folklore that munches on flames like a favorite snack..."

The instructor kept trying to light the kiln, the flame kept going out. As if the fire itself was scared to ignite.

After classes, Windy was alone at a study table in the college library, as she was every day, several books in front of her, pretending to read.

"But at this point in my tale, by knowing that, you know more than me: I suppressed the memory of the first two rounds of my epic battle against fire. This is the story of Round Three."

One of the books in front of her just happened to be a vintage English language book: *Tales of Old Corea* in the archaic nineteenth century spelling. But Windy had pulled this off the shelves randomly, it did not yet have any special meaning for her.

"The old folk tales don't just begin with a formula, they always end with one. Like 'And they lived happily ever after'—which we say in Korea and pretty much everywhere else. Though in some places they just say 'The End.' Period. Not sure which one is going to apply in my case."

Her watch buzzed the time. She stacked the books.

"We'll both find out if you decide to stick around. But I won't hold you to it. The thing about myth is that you can come and go as you please, it will always be there."

Then she carried the stack to an older woman librarian to check them out.

"You certainly are an avid reader," said the woman, recognizing her.

"Yes, ma'am," Windy answered, with a genuine smile.

"See you tomorrow."

"Thank you."

"I have no interest in ceramics or in education. I'm dyslexic. Reading literally hurts. So I don't. Unless my life depends on it. But my mom worked in this library, right here at this desk. And so that's why I applied and got accepted and otherwise waste my time at this college. Because I can spend every afternoon in the library and pretend this is her checking out my books and smiling at me and telling me to have a nice day."

Windy shoved the half dozen books into her backpack.

"Goodbye," said the librarian.

"Bye, Mom."

Whoops.

"Ma'am," Windy quickly corrected herself. And then headed for the door.

A half hour later, the bus stopped and Windy exited, heading toward the same modest Yaksu apartment building where she had lived for the past twenty-four years. Along the way, she passed a street vendor making and selling corndogs, crossing in front of a woman in her late twenties who had just purchased two of them and seemed to give Windy a long and close stare as she went by.

"Yup. That hungry gal was definitely spying on me."

The woman, Hungry Gal Noh, stuck both corndogs into her mouth at once, and watched Windy continue on.

A limousine known as the Beast, a chunky, black Cadillac, solid as a block of granite—the same design as the vehicle that hauls the President of the United States around Washington DC—pulled to the curb near the vendor. A young man, PJ Kwon, stepped out. He was in his late twenties, street stylish and very handsome. He moved over to Hungry Gal and they both watched Windy disappear into the nearby apartment building.

"Is she really one of us?" said Hungry Gal between bites.

"Who knows?"

"Well, if we did know," scowled the young woman, "we wouldn't have to camp out here all hours of the day and night, would we?"

"What else are we gonna do?" shrugged PJ.

"Get something to eat, for one thing."

"Doesn't seem to have stopped you," he said, eyeing the vanishing corndogs.

"I mean real food. In a restaurant. I want intestine."

"Go for it."

"Alone is boring."

PJ indicated the woman who now waited outside the Beast. She wore classic limo driver attire, was in her thirties, severely beautiful and just plain severe, in attitude and demeanor, expression as hard as the metal of the vehicle she controlled. "Why don't you invite Driver Park?"

"That's eating alone."

PJ considered how impenetrable the driver appeared. "You're not wrong."

"See you."

"Yup."

They parted ways, Hungry Gal Noh getting into the limo as Driver Park got back behind the wheel and pulled away from the curb, leaving PJ to glance back at Windy's apartment building. He did a couple of stretches, as if he was going to be there half the night ahead, watching the building—which was in fact, the case.

Windy entered the apartment to find her father and stepmother watching television as was their usual routine.

"Hi," she said.

"Hi, sweetheart!" said her father.

"Hello, dear!" said her stepmother.

Their greetings were forced. Both appeared cowed, as if perpetually walking on eggshells whenever Windy was around.

"My father of course, had been riddled by guilt ever since he left mom and me to the flames, hammering a nail in my heart for all time. He would do anything to

make amends, but I'll never forgive him. And as for her, I could sense the terror just below the fake smile. At this point in our tale, I still had no idea why."

Windy settled in on the sofa between the two of them, as if doing her best no matter what she did, however trivial, to make them uncomfortable.

"My very first memory is of my father's betrayal. How can I ever trust anyone again? So my han is extreme. Since han by definition is what you can't revenge your way out of, the most I could do is exploit the guilt and the fear to the max. With just one word."

"Chikin."

Her father and stepmother gave weak smiles of feigned excitement.

In a manner of minutes, a delivery motorcycle rider with a logo emblazoned on his jersey was whisking Windy's order across Seoul to her door. And a few minutes after that, Windy was digging in, her father and stepmother reluctantly doing the same.

"They will order chikin every single night for the rest of their miserable lives. And they will pretend to enjoy it."

Windy watched their tired eyes with zero empathy.

"At least, that's what I thought was going to happen. But as they say: 'Trend is not destiny.' My season of double-fried poultry in perpetuity was soon to be over."

"Once, in Finland, there was a little boy, whose mother loved him as only a mother can... a moody and sulky little boy, who will regret forever all the times he could have said, 'I love you' or even just smiled at her, but did not."

The adolescent boy in question was riding with his mother on a wooden sled pulled by a reindeer. They were in Lapland, 250 kilometers north of the Arctic Circle. There was no sound but the creaking of the wood and the breathing of the animal. A light snow blanketed the surroundings, but the sky was clear and the sun bright. The trees they were moving through looked like Christmas trees from a postcard: each exactly the same size and shape.

The woman tried to put her arm around the boy, but he moodily shrugged her off. As he always did. She smiled anyway. As she always did.

He did not know she was dying.

Suddenly, the boy noticed a massive shadow gliding over them, as if from an immense bird.

Then the sled stopped. It was just one among several, roped in a line for tourists. Two guides shouted in the Sami language, which the boy did not understand, having been raised with Finnish only. People converged on the boy's sled, surrounding his mother, who was clearly stricken.

He stood aside, watching them try CPR. Even then, when he finally realized something was wrong with his mother, his emotions seemed bottled up, inaccessible.

A rush of wings filled his ears. He looked up, squinting against the sunlight, and saw what looked like a gigantic black swan, the size of a passenger jet.

The great bird was singing a wordless song, filled with beauty and longing. It paused for a moment in midflight, then vanished.

"The boy saw the swan of Tuonela, the Finnish Land of Death, and heard its song. And his mother was gone."

Twenty-five years later, that same boy, Mathias Halko, now in his late thirties, strode along a busy city street in downtown Helsinki. He was handsome, professorial, a folklorist by training.

He repeated aloud to himself some lines in English, rehearsing. "Over one hundred years ago, a young girl wrote a letter to a New York City newspaper, asking: 'Is there a Santa Claus?' Over one hundred years ago, a young girl wrote a letter…"

He stepped into a large business hotel, passing a sign on a stand that read both in Finnish and English: "Welcome International Association of Folklorists."

A few minutes later, he passed a placard just outside the door of a conference room that announced his topic and himself:

"Yes, Virginia, there is a Santa Claus." Mathias Halko, Professor of Folklore Studies, Aalto University.

And a few minutes after that, he was at the podium delivering his talk in English: a continuation of what he had been rehearsing as he entered the hotel. Apropos of his chosen topic, he was wearing a red Santa-style hat.

"... And the now-famous editorial answered her with 'Yes, Virginia, there is a Santa Claus' after arguing that if there were not, life would be 'dreary' indeed." He paused to set up an obscure academic joke. "An *ad misericordiam* logical fallacy if ever there was one."

Which nobody laughed at.

Halko glanced up from the podium. Only half a dozen folklore professionals were in attendance, scattered among a couple of hundred empty chairs.

He soldiered on. "In between the everyday world of common matter that is perceived by our senses, and the world of pure ideas as perceived by the intellect, is a middle ground. An intermediate world, of image-idea, of archetypes. A place existing outside of the human mind and yet perceivable only by an active, directly willed imagination. This world has been called the Imaginal realm by those whose study is religious mysticism. I propose today that the Imaginal is none other than the field of action—the dwelling place, as it were—of the figures of myth and legend that populate human folklore…"

And so it went for the rest of the hour.

Halko concluded his talk with a call to arms, as it were. "…As folklorists, I suggest it is well past the time we acknowledge the reality of these figures. Creatures of myth and legend exist not just in our imaginations,but as real presences in the Imaginal world, able on occasion, of extending that presence into our own."

And again, he tried some humor. "So, yes Virginia, there is a Santa Claus—he just doesn't live at the North Pole."

And once more, there was no laughter. Indeed, the only remaining individual in the audience didn't even applaud. He was an older Finnish man, Halko's mentor of fifteen years.

Halko left the podium and went to meet him, indicating the empty chairs with irony. "Clearly, the International Association isn't ready for what I have to say."

But the older man was not in a joking mood. "There is so much to be done in our field of study: anthropological sourcing, comparative analysis, fieldwork if you wish to get your hands dirty. Write a book about memes, for goodness sake. But this nonsense?" He mixed Finnish with English, as did Halko.

"It's the truth."

"Because you say it is?" asked his mentor. "Show me evidence that even one 'Santa Claus' has climbed down even one chimney anywhere on this planet. Just one figure of myth and legend genuinely appearing and causing change in the real world. If you cannot show me that, then you are chasing faery dust and destroying what was once a promising career."

He turned away and exited the hall, leaving Halko behind. The scholar sat down in a chair, then suddenly remembered he was wearing the Santa hat. He went to pull it off, then decided to leave it on. Anybody else might have felt like a fool, but the rejection of his peers and his old advisor only further solidified his resolve.

The massive tiger that appeared once before has again entered our story. This time, it walked through the spacious, glass-walled entrance lobby of a high-tech office building that served as headquarters of the Titanis Corporation.

"Once, when Tigers smoked..."

Wisps of gray wafted away from its fur as the huge cat stepped into an elevator and turned to face forward, just as a human would, and the doors closed in front of it.

On the inside of the doors was a stylized logo of Prometheus, bringing fire down from the heavens.

"... There was a young man whose hero was Prometheus, the Titan who stole fire from the gods and gave it to humans, at great personal cost: specifically, being chained to a rock and having his liver eaten by a big eagle on a daily basis. The young man thought of himself as a Titan, and he too, wanted to be known— by everyone for as long as there is anyone – as the technological savior of humanity."

A charismatic engineer/CEO whom we will call Firestarter Kan, stood at the head of the conference table occupied by the board of directors of his company.

"The next step for Titanis is the next step for our nation and for humankind as well."

The stony-faced older members of the board of directors, seated at a large conference table, are evenly matched by the number of younger, "next generation" type of corporate executives.

"Our Fast-Push product not only increased download speed for smartphones by an order of magnitude..."

Titanis was one of a small handful of hotshot, high-tech start-up companies that had only recently started appearing in Korean industry, with all the birthing pains that might be expected when confronting established ways of doing business.

But Firestarter Kan seemed able to have one foot in each world.

"... It allowed breakthroughs in multiple, even unrelated industries: robotics, medical technology, materials sciences."

He was a visionary, but he presented things as rational and reasonable, whether they were or were not.

"Our newest product will accomplish what technologists—and dreamers—have long dreamt of: to make something from nothing."

Everyone looked at him. Suddenly, they all started spontaneously applauding, even those on the fence. Even if they didn't understand what he was saying. Only one man did not join in the enthusiasm.

"Our laboratories and development departments have not been actively engaged in the pursuit of such an... invention," said the doubter.

"The trips I have made in the past two years."

"Your holidays. To Europe, to the Amazon, to Siberia."

"Were anything but. I was engaged in research. And that work has paid off."

He indicated the multiple antiquities displayed in the glass cases lining the walls: terracotta figurines, bronzes, marbles.

"These... souvenirs," explained Kan, "were all used in shamanistic operations dating back tens of thousands of years."

"How is that relevant to what we are doing today?"

"What is old is new again. I do not intend to 'invent' our biggest breakthrough yet. But to acquire it by other means."

"What means?"

"That's proprietary," smiled Firestarter Kan.

"Even from us?"

"I only ask for your collective patience. And your trust. I have never failed you. I will not fail you now."

There was a moment of silence. Then everybody again applauded in a show of support. Even the doubter finally joined in.

A young man called Poet Jun for his Romantic and reverie-seeking inclinations, was seated at the bus stop in front of Windy's apartment building. He was in his early thirties, extremely handsome, and stared at the thin crescent moon, a contemplative smile on his face. Nobody else was around. It was late. And the busses were infrequent. One stopped; he made no move to get on, and it kept going.

Then Windy stepped outside of her apartment building. He was instantly on alert, watching her. He too, was one of the people "spying" on Windy. He raised his cell phone, centered her on his photo app, and magnified it to see her face: Windy's eyes were half-closed. She was sleepwalking.

Poet stood and positioned himself to shadow her movements, but then Windy abruptly turned around and went back into the apartment building. He smiled to himself.

In a large family room across town, an eating show played on the large screen TV. In front of it, Hungry Gal Noh, the two corndogs a distant memory, ate a bowl of instant ramen while scrolling through delivery options on her Samsung. An odd assortment of "family" occupied the room around her: ADMIN Yoon, a classic, accountant-type guy in his mid-thirties, worked a spreadsheet on his tablet; Kid Kee, midteens, was refurbishing an antique computer game console from the 1980s; PJ, who had relieved Hungry Gal at the stakeout in front of Windy's apartment, idly did pushups to keep in shape—he did Yudo in his free time, of which he had a lot, as did the rest of them.

Hungry Gal considered the mukbang as she ate: it was her favorite YouTube channel, an older couple and their twenty-something son, all dour faced—though that was undoubtedly for the camera—eating massive amounts of whatever the mom had fixed this week. The best thing about mukbang was to watch while eating, as she did now, because then it was like you ate twice. Or in the case of a show hosted by a small family, four times.

She turned to ADMIN Yoon, once again expressing her doubts about Windy. "You really sure she's one of us?"

ADMIN sat up straight, as if to distance himself from what he was doing on the tablet: rechecking his own work. "Of course. Genealogy doesn't lie."

"People make mistakes."

"I'm not 'people.'"

"Well, you got that right," Hungry Gal agreed.

The TV suddenly turned off.

Noh scowled. "I was watching."

"Forgive me," said Poet Jun, who had picked up the remote as he stepped into the room.

Everybody looked up at him, but without much anticipation.

"At approximately 9:47 p.m., Miss Windy Lee went for a little walk."

Everybody perked up.

"Fugue state?" asked ADMIN.

"Apparently."

"How long?" asked the Kid.

"Less than a minute outside. She turned around and went right back in."

"Told you so," said Hungry Gal. "She's just some chick who walks in her sleep sometimes. She doesn't belong here."

PJ got up from the floor. "Why are you so sure?"

"Women's intuition."

"You just don't want another girl in this house," said the Kid.

She threw a throw pillow at him but he easily dodged it. "It's the other way around. I welcome an ally against the likes of all of you."

Poet had a thoughtful expression on his face. "It's quite interesting. Like she's fighting it."

"Is that so weird?" countered PJ. He and Poet had a bit of a competitive dynamic between them. Or at the least, contrarian. What one said the other countered, and vice versa.

"Certainly some of us, myself included, cannot make the leap, as it were," admitted ADMIN.

"Because you're trying too hard," said Hungry Gal. "Not because you're trying not to."

"You always say that," said the Kid. "Nobody knows how this stuff works."

"I could see it on her face," said Poet. "As if she stood on the precipice. And the desire to step into the void was so strong that it froze her in place. And so, she did not."

"You imagined all that?" smiled PJ. "From across the street?"

Poet just looked at him. "I zoomed in with my phone."

Hungry Gal took the remote out of his hands. "That's so... creepy." She turned her show back on.

"At least I keep my distance. Unlike some."

Hungry Gal had indeed gotten right in Windy's face when she passed by the corndog stand.

ADMIN shook his head at the data on the tablet. "According to the principles of inheritance and genetic drift, Miss Lee should be one of the strongest of our kind in... well, in all of history."

The Kid was amazed. "No way."

"Come on," agreed Hungry Gal.

"If that's true then she should never be left alone," said PJ.

"Driver Park is there now," said Poet.

Hungry Gal shook her head. "We can't keep this up forever."

ADMIN closed his tablet. "Agreed. It's not sustainable. Perhaps it's time we force the issue."

Everyone glanced at him. He pushed his glasses up his nose in a slightly nervous gesture. "Any volunteers?"

Poet considered. "I'd take the job, but I might be spotted..."

"... And that pretty face of yours can scare people off," said Hungry Gal with a combination of admiration and annoyance.

Poet just shrugged. He didn't disagree.

"I'll do it," said PJ. "I'm not that pretty."

"I beg to differ," said Poet.

"Thanks. I think."

"In just the right light."

Hungry Gal scowled. "I won't be a part of this." She moved toward the large picture window and stepped out onto the balcony outside...

...to a spectacular view of Seoul. This curious band of people lived in an incredible mansion on a hill. A large, two-story, hanok-style home as designed by a modern urban architect, with balconies and a rooftop terrace. The view took in Gyeongbokgung Palace, Namsan Tower, the Han River, and points south.

To the east, in Jongno, was the massively tall superstructure of a building under construction: the "Tower of Olympus"—still an open and bare superstructure of steel—lit up in the night, the logo of Titanis Corporation bright enough to be seen from nearly anywhere in town.

The young woman on the balcony stared out at the city and her scowl faded, replaced with a look of heavy responsibility: as if the city was somehow her and her housemates' duty to protect.

"When Tigers did their thing, a brave young man almost died, trying to stop the same fire that killed my mother."

At the same fiery blaze that engulfed baby Windy's apartment building and changed everything about her life, a young firefighter was trapped beneath a chunk of wall, in a lower stairwell, the flames all around him.

He watched as the fire surrounding him suddenly made a leap in his direction as if pouncing—and then was violently drawn backwards away from him by some unseen, incredible force. As if yanked away by a tornado in another part of the building. But only the flames were targeted, nothing else felt the pull of this uncanny phenomenon.

"He never knew what happened that day. By what apparent miracle he was still alive."

The young man could not believe what he had just seen. The shocking sight overwhelmed for a moment even the tremendous pain in his lower body.

"But he swore he would find out..."

That same young firefighter was now Arson Investigator Kim—forties, wheelchair-using. He and his two-person team considered a large active monitor that displayed a detailed map of Seoul.

"... And he's still trying."

"The two largest fires in Seoul since I've been in business," commented Investigator Kim, "both in the last two months. Tens of billions of won in damage, no deaths."

He worked on an Android tablet with a stylus; the results were displayed on the large monitor, overlapping the map.

"Location number one," he continued, "Red Mirror office building, Gangnam. Location number two: White Boat parking structure, Hongik." He turned to his assistants. "Question is: Where do they strike next?"

Both of his aides reacted with surprise. "Investigator Kim," said First Assistant Choi, "you declared both those cases accidental."

"Officially and to the media," elaborated Second Assistant Cho.

"I lied," admitted their superior.

Again, his staff were taken aback. "To us, as well?" said Choi.

"There are more than enough cases of arsonists coming from 'inside the house,' as it were, from the ranks of fire prevention itself, to ignore the possibility," explained Kim. "I could not take that chance, forgive me."

"Why tell us now?" asked Cho.

Arson Investigator Kim wheeled himself over to the office door and locked it. "Because from now until the next fire, neither of you is to leave my side. Inform your parents and significant others you will not be coming home. Again, my apologies."

Before the pair could react, he tapped his Android and numerical and timecode data appeared on the large monitor. "At both locations: the times the fire alarms were activated versus the times the fire alarm systems registered smoke and flames."

Both assistants were astonished by this new bit of information

"Somebody pulled the alarm two minutes before the fire started," said First Assistant Choi. "At both sites."

"Which gave the public enough time to clear the area to safety," added Cho. "Result: no casualties."

"Zero. Both cases."

"Exactly," affirmed the investigator. "No casualties. Two major fires, potential for dead and injured extremely high. Even one fire with that outcome is very, very lucky."

"Two times in a row isn't luck," said First Assistant Choi.

Kim nodded. "It's intention."

The pair considered.

"What kind of arsonist wants to minimize the harm?" asked Cho.

"Not a terrorist," insisted Choi.

"Not a terrorist," agreed Investigator Kim.

Choi indicated images of the two sites in Gangnam and across from Hongik.

"I'd say somebody with a grudge against whoever owns or built the structures that were torched—but we looked at that. There's no financial or design connection between these two constructions."

"If the arsonists are sending some kind of message," admitted Cho, "I sure don't understand it."

"That's because we don't know what language they're speaking," said Investigator Kim, certain that was only a temporary lack of information. "Not yet."

The city of Seoul is positioned in a perfect geomantic setting: a valley between four mountains with a great river flowing across it. And on this particular day, it seemed even more lovely than usual: the sun brighter, the shadows sharper, the lines of the city exquisitely clean and clear. Almost unnaturally so.

Then a giant silken boot touched down in the middle of the wide boulevard in front of the Lotte department store in Myeongdong.

The boot belonged to Manshin Mae, professional shamaness, performing a gut ritual dance across the entire city to the sound of traditional drumming and fluting. The apparent giantess was beautiful and her costume a brightly colored arc as she swirled above the city. A thin handkerchief was tied around her eyes as a blindfold.

Then her dancing foot swept through a line of buildings – which let it pass through without effect: the entire city was a holographic projection, taking up a good piece of the floor of an airplane hangar owned by the Titanis Corporation. The mudang was very real however, as were the old flutist and old drummer accompanying her.

Firestarter Kan, the Titanis CEO, was at a computer console, documenting this performance with high-tech video cameras, motion capture and other advanced equipment that recorded more than just visible light, even what looked to be a seismometer just in case.

"Mythology was the way our ancestors made sense of events that were beyond their understanding." He spoke into a small microphone, in a low voice, unheard by the whirling shamaness, leaving a record in his own words of what he was doing for posterity, as an explanation of his illegal actions, and even as a manifesto: "If we substitute 'alternate universe' for 'heaven,' and 'aliens' for 'gods' then perhaps we get to the truth of what happened."

The mudang held a black dagger in one hand and a multicolored fan in the other, waving them as she danced.

"And more importantly, *what can happen again.* If advanced beings appeared to us thousands of years ago, bearing gifts of world-changing technology, then they can be invited to do so again. Invited. Persuaded. Even compelled if necessary. And if possible."

Manshin Mae appeared to be in a trance, her movements guided by nonrational impulses as she danced.

"It is simply a matter of opening the door between the universes, from our end," continued Firestarter Kan. "We cannot wait for them to take action. We must send the call. We must announce that we are ready. And to do so, we need only utilize the same methodology deployed by our ancestors."

The musicians played more insistently.

"Shamanism, that most ancient of human spiritual traditions, as practiced today in Korea, is also the most advanced."

Manshin Mae appeared to be circling over a location.

"The mudang's movements through space and time, informed by the ancient intuitions and knowledge of tens of thousands of years, serves as a gateway through space-time. Allowing information to move between the universes."

The music reached a climax.

"That is my hypothesis."

The dancer seemed to be ready to land on a place right below her twirling steps.

"It only needs to be tested."

Suddenly, the shamaness stabbed her dagger and fan together in a completely opposite direction of where the dance was taking her, coming to a stop with the stopping of the music as well, pointing to an unmistakable location in the miniature Seoul below her: a busy tourist area with a very large dancing fountain.

There it is, thought Kan.

And there he was, the next day, pacing around the huge, newly inaugurated fountain that had been constructed at the top of the main walking street in Insadong, to one side of the tourist welcoming center—the real-world location picked out by his hired mudang. He was accompanied by two henchmen, and they were all eating ice cream cones purchased from a nearby vendor.

The first henchman seemed disappointed at the surroundings, indicating the massive black stone base of the fountains. "Nothing but marble and water. No fuel."

But Firestarter was unconcerned. "When the obvious solution doesn't present itself, one waits for inspiration."

At that moment the regularly scheduled fountain show began: the water shot upward and began "dancing" to music. As the visitors all positioned themselves for the Instagram moment, the sunlight behind the fountain shined through the splashing droplets and appeared for a moment almost like flame.

Firestarter Kan smiled at the sight—and the similarity. "Just so."

Windy stared out the window of the bus at the traffic below. The public TV monitor up by the driver showed the face of the man with the big plan—Firestarter Kan—exiting his shiny office building as reporters shoved microphones and cameras in his direction.

"... the Titanis CEO refused to confirm rumors of a new product launch, saying that such speculation was 'premature,' even as construction continues on the company's megatall new corporate headquarters..."

The news report showed the same extremely high superstructure in Jongno that Hungry Gal had seen from her rooftop.

As the bus stopped at a corner in Yaksu, Windy, without a glance at the TV, exited to the street, heading home with her backpack full of library books as she did at this time each day.

And as she went up the front steps to the entrance, PJ came out of the building, passing right by, avoiding her gaze. He need not have bothered: she didn't notice him. When he was in the clear outside, he seemed for a moment almost disappointed that she hadn't given him even a glance. Maybe he needed a haircut.

An elevator ride later, Windy was surprised to see a heavy, gold-colored business card stuck in her apartment door—which, to her even greater surprise, was unlocked.

She pocketed the business card, stepped inside, and was stunned to find the entire place has been emptied out: all of her father's and stepmother's things were gone, there was nothing left but her meager belongings and the piles and piles of books she had checked out of the library with no intention of reading.

"They apparently decided that if the baby bird won't leave the nest, the nest has to leave the baby bird."

Windy found a note from her father, written on a chikin

delivery napkin, that read: "The rent is paid until the end of the month. I'm sorry."

Windy frowned, angry, but was close to tears.

"And so once again, my father abandoned me to the flames. Literally."

At a loss, she just stood there for a moment. Then she left the apartment in a kind of blur.

With nowhere to go and no one to be with, Windy took a bus back to the college and went into the library for the second time today, looking for the one familiar face she trusted—even if it was just a fantasy about her missing mother.

But instead of the librarian a young man sat in her place. Windy approached. "Excuse me."

"Yes?"

"Where's the lady who usually sits here?"

"Lady?"

"She was literally here just this morning. The librarian." Windy's voice was panicky. "She's here every day."

"Oh. Leave of absence."

"What?"

"Some family emergency, they said. But I can help you."

Windy moved away without responding, as if her last anchor to the world had been cut loose.

"Then I remembered the card."

She pulled out the business card that had been stuck in her door. It glimmered like... on a sudden whim, she bit into it.

"Because that's what you're supposed to do to test if it's real gold."

Her teeth left indentations as clearly as they would have in a dentist's wax bite block. She was amazed. Then read aloud: "Club H. Miss Windy Lee. You are invited."

She quickly worked her smartphone.

"Of course, I Navered them: 'Oldest and most exclusive private club in Seoul...'

"... By invitation only..." said ADMIN, repeating word for word the info that Windy had found on Naver.

She had texted the number on the card, and been persuaded by the person who responded to meet "the members" at a pojangmacha on a street in Jongno just to the south of the recently gentrified Iksondong neighborhood. But there was nothing "developed" about the row of orange, squarish tents, plastic chairs, and cheap drinking food that lined this street in the shadow of the huge under-construction Titanis building that loomed above them. It was one of the few places in the city where the pojangmacha still appeared in significant numbers when the sun went down. Windy thought that was the last place anybody could get away with kidnapping or otherwise offending her, so she got on the subway and went, finding the members of Club H at the fourth tent from the near end of the row.

Windy stood at the table where ADMIN Yoon, Poet Jun, PJ Kwon, Hungry Gal Noh and Kid Kee were sitting, already, it appeared, on their second or third round of soju and beer.

"No more than half a dozen members at any one time," continued ADMIN. "And yes, the business card is solid gold."

An auntie/owner worked the stove and small grill, despite having trouble keeping the charcoal lit, and the way she shot smiles at Poet and PJ annoyed Windy for some reason. It's not like she knew these people at all, but she felt immediately protective of them.

Still, she didn't sit down.

Without waiting for her to do so, ADMIN launched into the rundown for the potential inductee. "All your living expenses are covered, as well as a daily cash allowance; monthly deposits will be issued—to provide for your retirement, of course."

"Of course," echoed Windy.

She thought about her father's note saying the rent had been paid for one month, then cautiously lifted an empty shot glass. The Kid stood to reach it and poured from a soju bottle.

"What are you, like ten years old?" asked Windy.

"Fifteen," the boy answered. "And I'm the longest-serving member of this club."

Windy seemed confused.

"It's true," ADMIN jumped in. "He was inducted practically from birth."

" 'Longest 'serving'?" quoted Windy.

"We perform civic duties on occasion," answered ADMIN.

"Like charity work?"

Hungry Gal just laughed. She didn't want to be there.

"Did I say something funny?" asked Windy.

But nobody answered.

"The two super-cute guys barely said anything. But when you look like they did, I prefer it that way. I tried not to stare at them."

Driver Park, last seen behind the wheel of the beefed-up limo, was seated alone at a nearby table. As if she preferred her own company—or to keep watch.

"Why me?"

Everyone else continued eating and drinking while the ADMIN pulled a sheaf of documents from a briefcase: ancient scrolls and manuscripts; five-hundred-year-old slender books written in classical Chinese and a couple of obscure alphabets; notebooks from the twentieth century, and a tablet from a few months ago.

"Please, sit down."

"It's a little premature for that."

The oddness of her just standing there didn't seem to even register on the others, they just took her weirdness in stride. As if taking weirdness in stride was an occupational safety measure.

"As you prefer." Yoon's finger traced the connections down all the different sources. "Our lines of descent go all the way back to Baekje. Almost two thousand years. And so does yours."

"Royalty?" asked Windy.

Everybody smiled.

Hungry Gal laughed again. "I'm a princess and don't you forget it."

"I don't understand."

"On rare occasions a royal or two," explained ADMIN. "Mostly not."

Windy pointed to the names on the long list. "So what's the connection? Between all these people?"

"Friendship. Plain and simply."

"That's lasted two thousand years?" said Windy in disbelief.

"The ancestors invested well. Stayed out of dynastic politics. Remained faithful to nothing but each other. All of us represent the current end points of those lines of descent."

He showed her images of a dozen different "clubhouses" down the centuries—of paintings, woodcuts, photos—some were now ancient ruins.

"They always had a meeting place. Our present-day home is but the latest in that tradition."

Windy stared at the images; her lifelong mistrust told her this could not be the entire story. "I don't believe it."

Hungry Gal poured for herself and took two quick shots of soju in a row without bothering to wait for anybody else. She blurted out, "We're all Haetae, okay? When there's a big fire, we put it out."

Everybody else was annoyed that she had spoken up so bluntly. Windy considered all of them. Then laughed. "Like the snack logo? The guy on the bags of chips?"

ADMIN Yoon seemed embarrassed. He answered in a more subdued voice. "Yes, like the snack logo."

Windy gave a long, tired sigh. She tapped her shirt pocket with the business card inside. "Solid gold?"

"Yes."

"Well, I'm not giving it back."

PJ suddenly turned to her. "Every one of us went sleepwalking before we knew how to walk."

Windy stopped. Considered him for a long moment. "Me too."

But she still didn't sit down.

ADMIN was encouraged regardless, and quickly followed up. "It's called a 'fugue state.' A psychogenic condition that sends us out into the city in a semiconscious status and leaves us open to hosting a Haetae. An entity that is normally not capable of visiting or taking action in our world. As though we were natural mudangs, without need of ritual or ceremony to invoke its presence."

He let all that sink in for a moment. "Do you think... that has ever happened to you?"

Windy just looked at him. And was struck by rapid-fire memory images:

—The blaze around her when she was a baby.

—The flames on the balcony when her stepmother tried to burn the photos of her mother.

—Her pupils going shockingly wide.

"No," she answered calmly, quickly suppressing the memory of those events. "No. No, it hasn't happened to me."

"Then why do you have to say it so much?" wondered Hungry Gal Noh.

"Hey. It's okay," said the Kid. "We're all here. For each other."

The words seemed empathetic beyond his years. Windy's mistrust momentarily abated. Everybody smiled supportively at her—except Noh who just looked away.

But Poet was staring at the charcoal fire of the grill that the owner of this pojangmacha had going right next to them. His expression was mysterious and open at the same time—Windy tried not to find him attractive, but it didn't work.

He picked up the owner's fire iron and stabbed at the charcoal: it sent up sparks, which prompted a memory in him.

"When I was a little boy," he said, already in a kind of reverie, "my grandmother would poke at the hearth, when the fire had burned low..."

Windy was instantly swept along by his memory, as he again pushed at the logs.

"She would say to me, 'Look, child, the fire-birds are taking flight'..." At those words, sparks leapt up from where the iron landed, seeming to wing their way into the air, like tiny birds of flame.

Windy was entranced.

"I watched them fly..."

Windy, too, watched the tiny sparks ascend.

"And then vanish..."

The sparks disappeared as they burned out in midflight.

"Somehow go somewhere else, somewhere I couldn't see." He poked at the fire again, and again the "fire-birds" appeared. "Sometimes, I wanted to join them. In flight."

Windy saw nothing but the tiny sparks, which filled her field of vision as Poet's voice gently lulled her... "To wherever it was they went. When they went away. Taking my fear with them."

And she drifted off, even where she stood. And dreamed.

Of the prehistoric landscape of ancient Korea, with rolling green hills, streams of water, and megalithic dolmens stacked like tables: two or three tall pillars of stone atop of which lay a huge horizontal boulder. The tiny "fire-bird" sparks from the pojangmacha's burner moved through this atmosphere—but now they were flame-like butterflies, lovely and delicate.

Suddenly, shockingly, the gaping, muzzle-shaped mouth of a large creature leapt into view, snapping down on a bunch of butterflies—dispersing them.

Windy barely got a look at the fantastical animal's face: like a combination of lion and rhino, smiling as always. It was a Haetae.

And another *snap!* of the massive jaws ended the dream.

Windy woke with a start. She was still standing at the table in the pojangmacha. The sun was going down. The others were gone. She was alone at the table. Disoriented, taken aback by this odd turn of events, Windy turned to the owner. "Let me guess. They stuck me with the check."

"Paid in full."

An hour later, Windy was alone in the empty apartment, seated on the bare floor, surrounded by the books she never intended to read, having eaten a box of fried chiken by herself. It was still early in the evening, but she was very sleepy after this long and strange day. Windy nodded off for just a moment.

And a flash of the Haetae leaping at the speck of fire instantly filled her mind.

Windy woke with a shock and was suddenly on her feet, panicky. This was not what she wanted to see when she closed her eyes.

She went to the pantry and found a cardboard box her father had left behind: inside were an old chain, three padlocks, bungee cords, hammer, nails, and the home equivalent of gaffer's tape.

It only took a few minutes to seal the front door shut with all of those items: looping the chain around the doorknob and securing it with the padlocks, laying on the tape, crisscrossing with the bungee cords, nailing the door to its frame.

Satisfied and exhausted, she stretched out on a blanket on the floor and was fast asleep among the unread books.

In another time zone on another side of the world, Finnish folklorist Mathias Halko was also surrounded by books, but they constituted his home library and had all been read and reread. He ignored them now, and scanned his Nokia instead for the headlines around the globe, as was his habit. Landing on an online, English-language, Hong Kong based newspaper, something caught his attention: "Another Seoul Fire." Curious, he clicked the link, then skimmed the article from a few weeks ago, reading aloud to himself the part he found intriguing: "... this makes two major Seoul fires in as many months... in both cases, despite considerable damage, no casualties were reported."

He considered this, curious enough to take it another step. He did a search on "Seoul Fires." Found a bunch of postings. He clicked on "English language only" and read through them quickly: "Damage estimated at tens of billions of Korean won..." "Nobody killed..."

Nothing was of great interest there. He was about to go to something else, but one last post caught his eye: "So who put out the fires?"

Halko considered that. He did another search, this time allowing Korean language postings to show up as well as English. He found a message thread in Hangul, highlighted the first message, then copied and pasted it into Google Translate, translating to English:

"My sister's husband's cousin is a firefighter. He says the fires were out before he did anything."

Halko reacted. Went further into the thread, did the same copy/paste/translate operation:

"Yeah, both fires were already extinguished when they got there. Couldn't say that to media because WTF!!!!!" "Maybe it was Haetae! LOLOL"

Halko considered that, then went to his library shelves. He looked for a while and finally found what he was looking for: "Folktales of Old Corea"—the same book Windy had randomly checked out of the library in Seoul.

He opened to the index, ran his finger down the columns, and found "Haetae page 47," which took him to the lion-dog creature of Korean legend. The woodcut reproductions and drawings were simple but compelling. He read: "It is said that the Haetae consume fire as though it were a delicacy. And by so doing, have saved Seoul from conflagration for as long as there has been a Seoul. And even before."

He closed the book, his mind racing. "How fortuitous," he said to himself in Finnish. Excited, he grabbed his phone, quickly located the site for Korean Airlines, and made a reservation for himself.

Windy's snoring filled the dark, nearly vacant apartment. Then the snoring seemed to segue into something that sounded like a snuffling lion.

And she was on her feet, eyes half-closed, sleepwalking toward the door.

When she reached it, she paused at the multiple ways she had sealed herself in an hour or so previously. Her neighbors heard a violent, smashing chomp. But they ignored it, and nobody came out of their apartment to see that Windy's door had been bitten open from the inside, shattering the steel chain and padlocks and nails and tape and the wood of the door itself.

Moments later, Driver Park, standing outside her limo, spotted Windy, walking in a daze away from her apartment building. "She's in a fugue state," Driver Park reported on her phone.

"Any idea where she's going?" responded ADMIN.

"Not yet."

Windy suddenly made quick turns into a couple of alleyways, went up a number of concrete steps along a narrow street and vanished into the entrance of an underground subway stop.

Driver Park again reported in. "Yaksu Station." And followed Windy down into the station, trying not to lose her in the throng of commuters.

ADMIN Yoon spoke with her from the clubhouse library. "Understood. Stay with her."

He glanced up; the others—PJ, Poet, Hungry Gal, Kid—were all hovering in the doorway, waiting for the news and for their next move. "Let's go."

Halfway across the city, a silver-colored fuel-carrying tanker truck was moving faster than was safe for its size, as though on a mission.

The driver was the Titanis Corporation's CEO, Firestarter Kan; the passenger was one of his henchmen. Firestarter raised a cellphone. "ETA in twenty-three."

The other henchman walked among the evening crowd in Insadong, heading toward the dancing water fountain that had become a siren call every night for the Instagram crowd. "Copy that," he answered on his own cell.

The fountains suddenly activated according to their timed schedule, and everyone present couldn't help but ooh and aah at the pretty spectacle: multiple streams of water shot high into the air as dancing arcs and dazzling night rainbows. Up came the smartphones as everybody took their selfies.

Firestarter slammed on the brakes—stopping just in time as the traffic ahead of him jammed. His henchman cursed, but Firestarter stayed calm. "Everything is on our side. Believe it," he said, feeling himself protected by destiny.

Driver Park's unflappable cool stayed that way, even as she momentarily lost sight of Windy and had to run to find her again: just as sleepwalking Windy boarded a subway train and the doors closed before Park could follow.

"Where are you?" she said to her cell.

"Stuck in traffic," came ADMIN's reply. PJ was next to him, behind the wheel of a Genesis SUV, and the rest of Club H were all inside. They were in the same jam-up that Firestarter had run into.

"Don't lose her!" shouted the Kid over ADMIN's shoulder.

"Too late," said Driver Park, as the subway train left the station. "She's on Line 3 north."

"Any idea where she's going?" ADMIN asked to all in hearing distance, not just Driver Park. "Anybody?" As the traffic jam started to open up.

"Anguk Station," said Poet without thinking about it.

Everybody in the SUV turned to him, saw the slightly dazed expression. "I feel it," he added.

"Me too." It was Hungry Gal. Her eyes had gone hazy as well. "Insadong."

PJ didn't wait, trusting completely their intuitions: he gunned the engine and jumped across a median line to take the SUV in the opposite direction.

Windy, standing at one end of a subway car, appeared to be asleep, eyes barely open and pupils rolled back in her head, gripping the strap above her head. There were a dozen or so other passengers, all seated, all minding their own business.

"Dongguk University, this stop is Dongguk University," said the PSA voice of the Seoul Metro, first in Korean then in English—a holdover from the 1988 Olympics that never went away.

The subway car came to a stop and almost everybody else got off; nobody got on. As it took off again, the sleeping Windy was alone with three young thugs.

"Once upon a time, there was a young man who heard a story that began: 'Once upon a time, there was a bluish wolf with a destiny written by Heaven itself...'"

Thug #1 had indeed dyed his hair a blue tinge, honoring his mythical inspiration.

"That wolf was the ancestor of none other than Genghis Khan, fiercest conqueror in all of human history. I have to specify 'human' because we will soon need to expand our story parameters to include the presences of the non-human and the supra-human and the wish-they-were human and the so-glad-they-aren't-human and so forth. And so the young man thought that he, too, being a merciless, modern-day warrior, must have had a blue wolf for a relative way back when."

"Lucky!" said the tough young man in question in heavily accented English.

But Windy didn't hear that or see that. Her blurred vision showed her a faded image of the inside of the subway car superimposed over something else that seemed much more immediate: *The same ancient mythological landscape of green hills and dolmen megaliths that appeared in her earlier reverie at the pojangmacha. The sound was of a gentle wind.*

Windy snored in time with it.

"She sounds like my uncle," said one of the junior thugs.

The three young men continued to observe her, as more subway stops and riders came and went, until finally they were again alone with their intended victim.

"Next stop, Anguk Station."

As if given permission by the three-minute transit time to the next stop, the thugs all stood and moved toward Windy.

Her snore started to sound like a deep growl as they neared, the kind that might come out of a huge mastiff or a lion.

The thugs were caught off guard. Thug #1 barked out a laugh, but the others were suddenly unnerved, and they held back. Thug #1 continued closer. Again, the growl came out of the young woman's mouth, in such utter contradiction to the apparent source that it was almost surreal.

"Leave it alone," said Thug #2.

"Let's go," said Thug #3.

But Thug #1 didn't care. He stepped in front of her, held out his hand and waved it right in Windy's sleeping face, trying to get a reaction. Then he slapped her cheek to wake her up.

Suddenly, the low growl became an awful roaring snarl and there was a flurry of action, so fast it was hard to see what had happened, but the thugs glimpsed massive jaws opening impossibly wide, rows of wicked triangular teeth, and jarringly, a kind of smile... then CHOMP.

A long swath of arterial blood splashed across the window from inside the subway car, as it came to a stop at the next station.

Moments later, the doors opened, Windy stepped out, dotted with blood, still in the fugue state. Behind her in the subway car came screams of agony and terror.

The gleaming tanker truck wheeled into a service alley alongside the row of buildings behind the dancing fountain, then backed up to a bunch of water pipes with locked chains around their control valves. The two men jumped out, and Firestarter Kan broke the chains with a bolt cutter as his henchman grabbed the thick hose off the back of the fuel tank.

The two arsonists finished connecting the thick fuel hose from the tanker onto the water main. Firestarter cranked the water valve to open: the fuel in the tanker truck was now flowing into the water system which supplied the fountains.

The other henchman was milling around with the crowd in front of the water display, who were all waiting for the timed show. His phone rang and he raised it to his ear.

"Now," came the voice of his employer.

He clicked off the phone and moved swiftly to a fire alarm on a nearby wall, cracked the cover glass and pulled the lever.

The fire alarm sounded, blasting through the complex. Everybody looked confused, then concerned. Some started walking and some running to exit the area. Others just milled around: Maybe it was a mistake?

At the nearest fire station an alarm klaxon pierced the air. In response, firefighters pulled on gear, slid down poles and jumped onto firetrucks, which roared out of the station, sirens blaring.

Windy had sleepwalked from the subway station to the tourist information center. People were running into the street, fleeing the fire alarm. She continued along, wading through them like going upstream.

Driver Park had put the Beast into a crawl in front of the huge fountains. She spotted Windy, instantly pulled to the curb, jammed the limo into park, opened the door and jumped out, running and talking on the phone at the same time. "Got her."

"We're right behind you," came ADMIN's voice over her phone.

The driver pushed her way through the onrushing crowd and the continuous sound of the fire alarm.

But there were no flames. No smoke. Nothing.

And the shouts from the crowd underlined that mystery: "Where's the fire?" "What's happening?" "I didn't see anything!"

Windy deftly threaded her way despite her somnambulant condition. Driver Park approached, kept an eye on her, but kept her distance: following, but doing nothing to stop or to "rescue" her or even to wake her up.

The firetruck roared around a corner and blasted up a busy street down the middle of the lanes, siren blaring. A second truck immediately followed, adding to the sense of alarm and danger.

At the access alley, Firestarter shut the water pipe valve, blocking any more fuel from the tanker into the water system. He tapped his cell phone. "Now."

His henchman on the other side of the complex clicked off his phone and lit up a cigarette. He was standing above a thin channel that brought water toward the fountains that were a few meters away: one of dozens of such elegant channels.

But an opalescent shimmer now ran in the channel. It was no longer water, but liquid fuel.

The man took another drag on the cigarette until the tip glowed brightly. He let it fall into the narrow channel.

The fuel instantly caught fire, then ran like a burning fuse toward the fountains.

Windy was still sleepwalking through the fleeing crowd as the fire alarm continued and the fountains kept dancing.

Suddenly, the fountains ignited, each jet and stream turning to fire, the flames dancing in the exact same pattern as the water it replaced.

Everybody gasped. It was both terrifying and beautiful. Despite the danger, dozens took selfies and struck poses.

Poet and Hungry Gal stood nearby. They had just arrived on the scene, and were now watching, entranced by the spectacle.

The firetrucks roared up to the nearest curb and the firefighters spilled out, then stopped in their tracks. Even they were amazed and momentarily taken aback by the fire fountains. Despite years and even decades in the service, nobody had ever seen its like before.

It was a few seconds of that before it all went to hell: the streaming jets of fire wavered back and forth, loosely, then more wildly, like a puppet coming undone from the strings that controlled it, or tamed tigers suddenly going mad on stage.

Then the fountains exploded: fire shooting everywhere.

The fire captain bellowed to his company to move. Everybody bolted into action, running towards the fire, dragging water hoses, shouting encouragement to keep their courage up in the face of this bizarre apparition.

Still in a fugue state, Windy Lee walked calmly towards the fire, like the proverbial moth toward the flame, but with the moth having the advantage...

Then, in a moment of frozen time, her pupils filled the whites of her eyes, just as they had when she was a baby facing a fiery death in her parents' apartment.

Suddenly, reality shifted, and overlaid across this view was the green, dolmen-dotted Neolithic landscape. In the distance, a blast of fire roared up from the ground, as though from a minivolcano.

She felt herself running across this landscape, and unseen figures of what sounded like a wolf pack or a pride of lions were running alongside her. In fact, she seemed to be in the lead position.

Windy glanced to one side and recognized the lionlike

muzzle, the big jaws, the iron horn on its head, the thick, immensely powerful body:

Haetae. Of course it was smiling at her.

"I felt like I was among friends. Even family. For once in my life. And the prospect was so shocking and so exciting that it woke me up."

"Sorry, guys!" shouted Windy, feeling the need to apologize for leaving them. The mythological scene suddenly dissolved away and the Haetae vanished along with it, evaporating like a dream.

Windy had left the fugue state, and was now standing in the middle of the actual blaze, surrounded by flames, and in great danger of being burned alive.

"Get out of here!" It was Hungry Gal, moving forward into view, eyes glassy, but still conscious enough to be simultaneously pissed off at Windy and warn her to safety. Then Hungry Gal opened her mouth, and superimposed over her was a Haetae.

Windy watched in amazement as it opened its jaws.

Then the flames rushed toward it as if being pulled against their nature, as if being dragged into a black hole. The noise was what would happen if fire could scream—in agony or ecstasy, Windy could not tell.

Then, everything seemed to happen at once:

—The original source of the fire at the fountain had been snuffed out.

—The Firefighters were stunned. "What?" "Backdraft?" "What the hell?"

—No sign of the Haetae.

Poet rushed to support Windy, PJ did the same for Hungry Gal, and they quickly helped the two disoriented women away from the scene, their actions and presence hidden from public view by all of the smoke.

As Firestarter and his henchman tried to finish securing the hose to the truck and get out of there, a voice broke through the drifted smoke.

"Hey!" Arson Investigator Kim rolled up in his chair, flanked by his two assistants. "How y'all doin'?" Belying his casual tone of voice, the assistants were already running toward the tanker. The arsonists jumped into the cab and Firestarter jammed it into motion. As the vehicle took off, Investigator Kim saw the hose at the back of the tanker suddenly come loose: the arsonists had been interrupted before it could be properly secured.

He did a quick mental projection of the most likely scenario, pulled out a radio, called in an alert on the tanker truck, then told the dispatcher the path of least resistance for such a vehicle, advising police to close off the side streets and set up a blockade before it reached a large square five kilometers away. "Send all available firetrucks to that location."

A voice responded, "Confirmed."

As the tanker sped away from the scene, the metal nozzle of its hose bounced along the asphalt of the street, just as Inspector Kim surmised it would.

Firestarter was driving as fast as possible, but traffic forced him into making turn after turn after turn, until he passed beneath a sign that named the same boulevard predicted by the arson investigator.

In a few moments, the CEO saw police cars coming toward him at high speed from all possible angles: flashing lights and sirens and shouting from bullhorns.

Then he glanced in his side-view mirror and saw the metal nozzle smacking the street, and the sparks it made as a result. His eyes went wide. He slammed on the brakes. The fuel nozzle bounced one more time off the asphalt, one more shower of sparks that ignited what was left of the fuel in the hose.

The two men dove out of the cab of the truck as the tanker with its remaining fuel exploded with a tremendous blast.

The truck still had speed, despite the last-moment

braking. It roared majestically on fire up the boulevard and toward a blockade of police cars that had just been frantically driven into position in front of it.

The police officers abandoned their vehicles and took cover as the flaming tanker struck the cars and everything went up in an even bigger explosion.

The firetrucks that the arson investigator advised be sent there arrived and immediately trained their equipment at the conflagration.

On the sidewalk a block away from the smoking ruins of the fountain, Windy was still dazed, Hungry Gal had fully recovered, and they were now surrounded and aided not just by Poet and PJ but by ADMIN, the Kid, and Driver Park—all of whom rushed them toward the SUV across the street.

"What did I just see?" asked Windy, looking at Hungry Gal.

"The truth," she responded.

"About us, about you," added ADMIN.

"Does that include biting a guy's arm off on the subway?"

The others just looked at her, noticing for the first time that Windy's clothes were stained with a dark crimson.

She suddenly faltered as she went.

Poet and PJ both caught her, kept her on her feet and still moving.

"Not bad for a newbie," said the Kid.

"She panicked and bailed out," disagreed Hungry Gal. "I had to cover for her. Or she'd have been barbequed."

"It's always food with you," said PJ.

As they continued to haul Windy along, she started to feel faint. "I just want to go home."

Then she passed out, from the exhaustion and just plain uncanniness of her experience this evening.

"You heard the young miss," said Driver Park, like a command.

Arson Investigator Kim and his two assistants moved through the aftermath of the blaze as firefighters continued the mopping-up operation, and paramedics treated minor injuries and smoke inhalation. Amazingly, it appeared that not a single person was seriously injured let alone dead.

His radio buzzed; it was the police lieutenant's voice. "We're good here."

"That's good to know."

The lieutenant was amazed at how perfect the investigator's orders had been: the smoking pile of metal that was all that remained of the tanker truck and the police car blockade was no longer burning; there were no casualties; it all appeared safely contained. Thanks to the "prescient" ability of Investigator Kim to read a situation and correctly anticipate the outcome in a heartbeat. "Appreciate the heads-up," he added.

"My pleasure."

"We lost the suspects."

"All in good time," said Kim reassuringly into the radio.

"But there were no casualties," continued the police officer, barely believing it. "We got lucky."

"Here as well, no casualties. Thank you, Lieutenant. Kim out."

He clicked off the radio, again considering the scene and the noticeable lack of human consequences, despite the potentially—even spectacularly—destructive circumstances.

"Very 'lucky.' " But Arson Investigator Kim, as he never tired of stating, didn't believe in luck. Or anything else beyond the billiard ball caroming of the particles of the physical universe.

He turned to his assistants. "Let's have a look-see." Then he rolled deeper into the still-smoking scene of destruction, his staffers moving to keep up.

The would-be "wolf" with the blue-tinged hair and a stump where his arm used to be was in an intensive care unit, wired up and unconscious.

His co-thugs stood nearby, still upset.

"A girl did this?" said a voice they were expecting. Boss Kang, the mobster they worked for, had entered the room. He was the boss of a very minor urban territory and as such tried never to make waves: any undue attention and he and his operation would have long ago been gobbled up by much bigger sharks in the sea in which he swam.

"She bit it off."

"Please don't say things like that."

The other thug had no choice but to concur with his colleague's report. "Sorry, boss. It's true."

Kang seemed pained by this situation. He turned to consider his fallen "soldier" on the bed, and his thoughts were colored by how much he hated his status as a low-level crime figure. A couple of small neighborhoods was all he controlled. The higher-ups in his world seemed to just tolerate him. His territory was not lucrative enough to take over, and he himself was not a threat to anyone. That being the case, this... *indignity*, to have one of his few men get his arm cut off—bitten off? don't be ridiculous—by a girl? It was too much to bear. If word got around, he would not just lose face, he might be attacked by an equally lowly rival, wishing, as Kang did, to pull himself out of the gutter.

"Let's find her," he said. "And clear all this up."

That night, Windy was asleep on the blankets on the floor of her abandoned apartment, snoring as usual.

"'And so it happened, and so it is,' as they sometimes say at this point in a tale."

Her new "family" was scattered around the small space—Poet, PJ, Hungry Gal, Kid, ADMIN—leaned against the walls, or curled up on the hard floor, all asleep.

Driver Park was seated with her back to the broken door, eyes closed but still keeping watch.

"'Whether it be truth or lie, take what you want, and give the rest back to me' is something they also sometimes say."

Windy suddenly roused and stood up, alarmed. Then she saw everybody crashed out like a lion family after a hunt.

Superimposed momentarily over that image in her mind's eye was the same scene out of the mythological world next door: all of them were Haetae, scattered around the base of a stone megalith, sleeping in the same positions as their human counterparts.

Comforted by the sight, Windy dropped back down to the floor and instantly fell back to sleep.

No longer alone in the world.

" 'But I hope it's true.' That's me saying that."

2. Middle

Motif Types

F770. Extraordinary buildings and furnishings.

F750. Extraordinary mountains and other land features.

F151.1.3. Perilous forest on way to otherworld.

F153.1. Underground channel to otherworld.

N512. Treasure in underground chamber.

A115.4. Deity emerges from darkness of underworld.

L420. Overweening ambition punished

F159. Other means to reach the otherworld.

T92.1. The triangle plot and its solutions. Two men in love with the same woman.

A173.2. Gods imprisoned.

F772.2. Metal tower.

D810. Magic object a gift

X1731.1. Person falls from great height without injury.

B37. Immortal bird.

Windy woke up to an empty apartment. Her abandonment issues instantly kicked in, manifesting mostly as anger. She called the number on the golden business card that she had already saved to her phone. ADMIN answered. "Why do you guys always take off before I wake up?" she said without identifying herself.

"We were trying to respect your space."

"Well, the rent on my space is up at the end of the month which is in two weeks."

"Your room is ready when you are."

Thirty minutes later, Driver Park pulled up to the Yaksu curb in the Beast. The corndog seller had been replaced by a dalgona candy cart which, in the wake of the success of *Squid Game*, had made a comeback of sorts on the streets of Seoul. Windy peered into the window. "I'm not getting in this thing. There's no way out."

"I could say the same," said the limo driver, without a lot of patience. "I'm not in the mood right now to have any of my limbs bitten off."

"I didn't do that on purpose. But point taken." Windy got in the car but insisted that the doors remain unlocked, and in fact, she kept the door at her side ajar so that she could see the surface of the street passing by as they went. Again, Driver Park, like the rest of her crew, did not think twice about this or any display of unusual behavior on Windy's part.

In Insadong, the investigation was just wrapping up after a full night and half the morning. Everyone was exhausted. Arson Investigator Kim was in the middle of thanking and dismissing his two assistants when a police officer stepped up and said, "I was told to tell you something."

"What might that be?" asked Kim.

The cop, as tired as the rest of them, ran him through the known details of the assault in the subway car, that somebody was maimed on the Orange Line between Jongno 3-ga and Anguk Stations. That the time was exactly when the fire occurred.

The arson investigator was intrigued. "What happened, exactly?"

"Somebody got their arm cut off."

"I see. Is the investigation still in process?"

The officer told him that it was, and took his leave. Intrigued, Kim turned to his assistants. "Let's check it out."

But both of his staff were tired. "What could it possibly have to do with the arson?" said First Assistant Choi.

"I'm sure nothing."

"Then why bother?" asked Second Assistant Cho.

"I'm sure of a lot of things that I'm wrong about." And so, rather than home to bed or somewhere for breakfast, they headed to the Metro stop, which was only a five-minute wheelchair ride away.

At the station, trains had been routed to parallel tracks, and the subway car where the incident had occurred remained in place, taped-off from public use. The police detective still on the scene took the arson team through the subway car. Blood was everywhere.

"Did the assailant have a sword?" asked Investigator Kim.

"Can't explain it otherwise," answered the detective.

"Where's the victim now?"

"Still checking the hospitals."

"And the arm?"

"The victim left it behind. Not enough to reattach, in any case. Pieces went to the coroner's lab."

Investigator Kim thanked him and turned to his bleary-eyed assistants. "Sounds like our next stop."

Windy rode the Beast up a hill in the Pyeongchang-dong district to the clubhouse, a hanok-style modern mansion of the sort she had never seen up close before. It was large enough to get lost in, and to hold secrets, even ancient ones. Driver Park guided Windy up a couple of sets of burnished wooden stairs to the rooftop terrace, where everybody was already eating a breakfast of rice and Jeju fish and soup and banchan. All of which had been prepared by ADMIN Yoon, who cooked when he wasn't doing something else, which was most of the time.

Windy stood at the table, as was her habit.

"Any questions?" asked ADMIN.

"Can we just eat first?" Hungry Gal Noh was annoyed. "Maybe she doesn't feel like talking."

"You just don't want to listen to her," said Kid Kee.

"That too."

"Fine with me," said Windy, as ADMIN filled her bowl and plate.

And so they ate. And never did get around to talking. And Windy never sat down.

When they were finished, Windy was guided by Driver Park to the bedroom that had been assigned to her. It was on the first floor, had a window covered in paper, a small writing desk and a sleeping mat. Windy thanked her, and in less than a minute after she was alone, was asleep, still in her clothes.

Dreamless sleep, a blessing for those with too much on their mind, was not to be hers this time around.

Windy dreamt of an old-fashioned ballroom and a masquerade ball, the kind that appear in European fairy tales, with everybody in big dresses and elegant suits and wearing Venetian-style masks. But rather than the traditional Italian Pantalone and Arlecchino, the elegant European guests wore the faces of the Hahoetal stock characters of rustic Korean folk performances. The juxtaposition was jarring. But Windy, as dreamers often do, didn't seem to notice anything unusual. Until an elegant hand reached out to offer her the next dance, and her gaze went up the ringed fingers, the tight black sleeve, the high collar to her would-be partner's face: the smile belonged to a Haetae.

The image shocked her awake.

She sat up. Got her bearings. Then tried to sleep again, too exhausted to let something so ephemeral as a nightmare keep her from taking a nap. If that even counted as a nightmare.

Arson Investigator Kim and his staff entered the laboratory in time to see a pair of medical professionals laughing as if Coroner Gil had just made a joke. He hadn't. "Get out. I'm not here for your amusement."

After the others had gone, Kim asked, "What did the gentlemen find so hilarious about a hard-working individual's conclusions?"

"Exactly. Assholes."

Investigator Kim introduced himself and his two assistants with proper respect, telling the coroner what they were looking for. Convinced his time was not going to be wasted, the man informed them about the serrations on the flesh of the detached and destroyed arm: "Less like a blade and more like a bite."

Second Assistant Cho tried not to smile, and under the quick but effective warning glance from his boss, tried harder.

"What kind of bite?" asked Inspector Kim. "As from a large dog? Like a mastiff?"

"Maybe. Or..."

"Or...?"

"Or a large cat."

"Larger than a house cat?"

"Much larger."

"Pick a cat. If you would."

"A lion." He knew how ludicrous that sounded even as he reluctantly said it.

"Thank you, Coroner Gil."

Outside the coroner's office, Arson Investigator Kim gave his assistants permission to go home, as Kim no longer considered them potential suspects, no matter how remote the possibility: they could not have been connected to the arsons since the inspector himself had seen the perpetrators in midcrime.

He told them that he was not going home to sleep because he had a shamanistic gut ceremony to attend. His staff reacted with surprise.

"You mean with a mudang and everything?"

"My sister is opening a new restaurant. She wants help from some cooking god or another." He said it matter-of-factly, with zero belief in the supernatural. Regardless, it was his view that to observe communal ritual events was simply being polite, and so, despite more than twenty-four hours of no sleep, off he went to the gut.

When Folklorist Mathias Halko arrived in Korea in the middle of the night, the taxicab that he hailed at Incheon International Airport had a cartoonish image of a Haetae emblazoned on its door. While not being a fan of Jungian thought, convinced as he was that folklore and myth were best characterized by local and unique differences rather than lumped into universal human archetypes, Halko nevertheless was as susceptible to the appearance of apparent synchronicity as everybody else. In this case, here he was, flying on a whim to Seoul, chasing a mythical monster that just might prove his cherished theories correct—and here was the thing itself as if to greet him! On the door of his taxi!

Had he known that depictions of the creature adorned not just taxicabs but bags of chips and that it was even the civic mascot of Seoul itself, he might have realized that its sudden appearance did not even qualify as a coincidence. But he did not. And so, fueled by that seeming serendipity, he had the driver drop him off right in front of Gyeongbokgung Palace, on one of the busiest streets in Seoul, where Google had told him that a pair of monumental Haetae statues stood guard.

He hauled his suitcase and his carry-on to the closest of the two, and gave it a self-conscious little bow. "Hello, Haetae-shi," he said, having found the "shi" suffix of polite respect on the language app he had downloaded only yesterday. "Thank you for welcoming me to your city. I hope we can find a way to work together."

A gaggle of tourists wearing rented hanbok traditional clothing gathered around the statue for pics—taking no notice of the folklorist and his impromptu greeting ceremony. But he took it as a signal to get going.

Exhausted and famished from his flight, he walked down the long and broad square stretching out from the palace, took a right at the huge statue of King Sejong the Great, and ended up in a twenty-four-hour mom-and-pop restaurant. He went in, got yelled at for not taking his shoes off fast enough, did so, then sat on the floor, arranging his luggage around him. He ordered the only thing he knew to say—bibimbap—and a bottle of soju spirits and a bottle of makgeolli rice beer, pointing at the bottles, as he had never seen their like before.

The soju seemed a bit like vodka-lite to him, and went to his head just as quickly. But the makgeolli! He recalled a Finnish tale, the daughters of nature who shed their salmon-hued milk upon the ground, from which iron sprouted. Was this then the elixir that made the Korean people like iron? Seemingly able to overcome all that history threw at them, no matter how vexing? And so the exhaustion and alcohol had stimulated the folkloric portion of his brain: the town square of synapses that filtered all life experience thru some old tale or another. Another bottle was in order. He ended up lying down on his bag—just to rest for a moment. And went to sleep.

Hours later, Halko was awakened by a slight kick from the female owner, as the first shift of neighborhood workers stopped in for breakfast at dawn. He had slept the entire rest of the night on the floor, undisturbed. Wanting to feel a kinship with the morning diners, the folklorist ordered breakfast as well—bibimbap, again—drank another bottle of makgeolli, then picked up his luggage, put on his shoes and walked off into the bright day to find a hotel.

A police detective paid a visit to Boss Kang at the latter's hagfish restaurant in Chungmuro. "Sorry about your guy," said the detective disarmingly.

"Things happen," shrugged the mobster, pretending to be busy.

"What actually *did* happen? On the subway car?"

"The boy slipped and fell."

"And lost half his arm?"

"It was a hard fall." The boss shoved both hands into a big plastic trashcan being used as a fish barrel and came up with a dozen live, slimy eel-like creatures, which he held in front of him. "Anything else I can do for you, Detective?"

The police officer tried another tack. "If this is the opening salvo in some little turf war, you could give me a heads-up. So my officers can be on the lookout for missing appendages in the days ahead."

"It's not. But thanks for the consideration."

The detective had known he wouldn't get anywhere with this interview. But it was his job to do it anyway. "You're welcome."

Then, almost as an afterthought, the detective smiled and shook his head. "The coroner said it looked like something chewed his arm off."

Boss Kang seemed to freeze a fraction of a second. Just enough for the cop to notice.

"That's ridiculous," he responded, as he dumped the hagfish back into the trash can.

"I thought so too." The detective left without saying goodbye.

Arson Investigator Kim's sister intended to open a golbangee restaurant in the neighborhood of Euljiro, which was the Korean equivalent of taking coals to Newcastle and she knew it, which was why she had hired the mudang: in an attempt to give her new establishment as much competitive edge as possible, even if that came from the supernatural side. And so in planning discussions between the shamaness and Kim's sister, they had decided, in addition to invoking the kitchen goddess which was a given, that since most of the whelks to be used in the restaurant's spicy salad would be fished off the coast of Wales, the gut would need to also propitiate the West Sea God, and because the owner of the previous establishment at this location—a tailor—had died while tailoring, his ghost had best be assured that nothing hinky would be going on here to tarnish his memory.

The investigator had been informed of all that, which for him, an avowed atheist, seemed the equivalent of trying to get in touch with Tinkerbell for business advice. He was here for moral support only, seated off to the side in his wheelchair, watching with zero interest as the mudang—much prettier than he had expected—started her ceremonial dance, accompanied by a pair of elderly musicians, whom he had heard were husband and wife.

But he could not help but take note of the details of the ritual itself: the flurry of colors and sounds and movements as the dance went on, the bright paintings depicting various mountain gods and ancestral shamanesses that had been taped to the walls. A painting of a tiger deity was hung by the entrance, appearing to both guard and welcome the proceedings.

The mudang very pointedly faced the four cardinal directions one after the other—south and north, west and east—gesturing and singing and shouting. Then she started to spin in the middle space between those four points, twirling long red ribbons that almost looked like flames...

As the shamaness was "possessed" by a sequence of otherworldly characters one after the other, Investigator Kim had a growing realization. After the gut ended, he congratulated his sister and introduced himself to the mudang as she was putting away her ceremonial objects, and they exchanged business cards.

As Kim exited the store, the shamaness received a phone call from the CEO of Titanis Corp, the man we know as Firestarter. This mudang was indeed Manshin Mae, the same shamaness he employed to dance across the holographic map of Seoul in search of the proper sites for his arsonry. "What does your schedule look like?" he asked politely.

In the empty hangar, Manshin Mae danced again. But this time, her dancing movements carried her spinning off the holographic reproduction of Seoul and onto the bare floor. At the controls of this simulation, Firestarter made some quick adjustments toward the east to accommodate the direction she had taken, and the holo-map extended accordingly, the landscape appearing under her feet as she went—and kept going, until her dance found their end point: in the middle of a forest halfway to the sea.

Arson Investigator Kim had called his staff away from their attempt to sleep off last night's all-nighter and into the office. The interactive map of Seoul had again been displayed on the monitor. Kim worked his stylus on the tablet as before, marking the map with photos of the first two arsons as well as yesterday's, walking them through the realization he had had at the site of his sister's new restaurant.

"First arson event, Red Mirror office building south of the river. The traditional element of the direction south is fire; the traditional color, red. The red vertical strips that make up the structure look like flames in the shifting light of day." Then he circled the next location. "Second fire, to the west: traditional element metal; color white. Arson site: a white-painted aluminum parking lot. And the third, last night's event. Element water, color black.

Direction north relative to the first two fires. Element water as evidenced by the water fountain hijacked to carry liquid fuel. The stone base of the fountain itself is black." He paused for a moment. "You with me so far?"

His staffers both nodded, still unsure of where he was headed. He waved the stylus toward the right side of the map. "The next event? Toward the east. Element wood. Color Blue. If they stick to the pattern they've established."

Second Assistant Cho looked overwhelmed and baffled. "What pattern is that, Investigator Kim?"

"It's a gut. The arsonists are performing a shamanistic ritual. Setting fires using the same symbology and directional positioning that mudang have used for centuries if not thousands of years."

There was a moment of silence. First Assistant Choi finally said, "If you say so, sir."

"I do say so. And so that's what we're looking for: east, wood, blue. Those are the parameters that the arsonist is trying to fulfil, that will tell us where he will set his next fire. Let's start searching."

Windy was disoriented, as happens when regaining consciousness in a place where one has never woken up before. The light from the window told her it was midafternoon, the comfortable mat and nicely appointed room reminded her finally that she was no longer in her own apartment. Then she smelled something... burning? No, *cooking*. And it made her realize how hungry she was.

She left the room and made her way along one side of the huge hanok, following the fragrance to a circular, brick-lined shaft with a wooden ladder that went downward into darkness. Hunger overcoming reluctance, she climbed down, amazed to find herself deep underground in an earthen basement, where ADMIN Yoon and Hungry Gal Noh hunched down around a very old stone circle with red hot rocks in the center. ADMIN cooked samgyeopsal, and Hungry Gal ate the pieces fresh off the iron the moment they became ready, not bothering to blow them any cooler than griddle hot.

"That smells so good," said Windy.

Hungry Gal indicated the circle. "Find yourself a good place to stand."

Windy did so, still not comfortable enough to sit down, and still wondering about the surroundings. "What is this place?"

"It *was* an altar to the god of the Earth," answered ADMIN. "Before our people were followers of Confucius, we were Taoists."

Hungry Gal scowled. "Come for the meat, stay for the lecture."

"Some of us have an appreciation for our origins. And how we got here—"

"I took the subway and two busses," said Hungry Gal. "As I recall."

"Metaphorically speaking."

"I don't speak in metaphors. Let alone eat them." She used chopsticks to pass a piece of meat to Windy, who took it with her own, dipped it in sauce, set it in the middle of a perilla leaf, rolled the edges together with one hand and ate. Incredibly, it seemed the best pork belly she'd ever tasted. But she wasn't going to admit that.

"Not bad," she said.

Hungry Gal just laughed. "Bullshit."

"Earth is receptive to Heaven," continued ADMIN as he cooked another round of meat. "When we go into the fugue state, we are like the mare in the *Book of Changes*, running tirelessly across the landscape. Having become the very embodiment of the receptive Earth principle."

He took a bite of meat rolled up in leafy greens. "Those of Heaven cannot move without

moving through a medium. No matter how powerful they might be. They need a channel into our world."

"That's us," considered Windy.

"Some of us, anyway," he said, with a tinge of

embarrassment. Then he explained. "I only *dream* of the Haetae. They have never manifested through me."

"Why not?"

"Genetic error? Unresolved psychological issues? I don't know."

"Maybe the Haetae come when they want to. Period. And it doesn't matter what our 'psychological issues' are." PJ had just dropped clear of the ladder and joined the conversation.

Poet was right behind him.

"Or perhaps Haetae just wants a partner to dance with," Poet said, as the two arrivals found places around the grill. "And they know you've got two left feet."

ADMIN blushed. "Well, I can't help that."

Windy instantly recalled the dream she had just had: the huge ballroom, the elegant dancers wearing the Bongsan masks, and the Haetae itself. Did Poet read my mind? she wondered, unable to keep herself from staring at him. He just smiled.

For the second place, Windy had directed Driver Park to her old neighborhood and her favorite Hof room, where she, the driver, and Hungry Gal drank draft beer and ate dried pollack. The other members of the Club had begged off. And it wasn't as though Hungry Gal had warmed much if at all to the addition of a new girl to their little group. It was just that she had a beggar in her stomach, as the saying went, and hated eating alone. So off the three had gone together.

Windy was surprised they hadn't already tried this place, since it was just up the street from where they had been spying on her. But Hungry Gal insisted that if she went inside every restaurant that looked like this one—average at best—she would be eating round the clock. Even she wasn't *that* hungry. That being said, she liked what she was having.

"Why didn't that little kid join us?" asked Windy.

"He went home for the day."

Home was where Kid Kee's parents lived, in Ilsan, about an hour to the west of Seoul. Their place was only modestly nice because with the money their son sent home every month, his mother and father preferred to be constantly on vacation: Jeju Island, Oahu, that Japanese winter onsen town featured in *Iris*, even Venice, Italy. The Kid had made no effort to keep his secret life secret from them—it was too much bother. As a result, they were his biggest fans. The place was filled with Haetae posters, Haetae statuettes, Haetae lamps, Haetae towels—there was no end to it. He loved his parents and his two younger siblings, but going home was exhausting.

Still chewing through dried fish and on another round of draft beer, Windy took leave to pay a visit to the restroom, the entrance to which was outside the restaurant and up a flight of stairs. When she came back down, she could see through the window that Noh and Park were busy with their meal, not missing her at all. She decided to pay a visit to the old apartment five minutes away.

Whether her intuition had told her this would be the case or not, sure enough, her father was already there, claiming he had forgotten something.

"Yeah. That you have a daughter."

"That's the only thing I'll never forget."

"Try hypnosis."

"I don't *want* to forget. You're all I've ever done that I still like." Was he speaking honestly because her stepmother wasn't there? Or did he just want to get out of the conversation as easily as possible?

Windy defaulted to the latter, indicating the empty apartment around them. "You took everything and left without even texting."

"You can take back whatever you need."

"I don't want any of your junk."

"I just couldn't turn down that much money."

Windy was caught off guard. "What money?"

The truth came out; her father was paid a backpack full of cash to leave.

"Who gave it to you?"

"Some kid."

"Same height as me, fifteen years old, maybe a Haetae on his t-shirt?"

"How did you know?"

Windy was furious at the betrayal. "I'll bite that little shit's arm off."

Her father was confused by the oddly specific physical threat. Then alarmed when Windy suddenly slumped against the countertop.

"Sweetheart are you okay—"

Windy straightened up, eyes glassy. Her father instantly recognized the sleepwalking condition he had seen since she was a baby. He tried to put himself in front of the door to keep her from going outside, but as she moved toward him, he heard a low growl that he had never experienced before. Shocked, he stepped aside and watched her go.

Back at the Hof, the women were ready for the third place. Hungry Gal checked out nearby dining options on her phone. Driver Park glanced out the window. "She's late."

Hungry Gal suddenly seemed to know there was a problem. "Shit."

Windy's Kakao app buzzed with an incoming call as she took an escalator down into the nearest subway station. Her face was the same combination of blankness and intention that seemed to be the rule for the fugue state. Of course, she did not answer or even seem to perceive the buzzing of her phone. In a few minutes she was inside a crowded subway car, standing with her hand in an overhead grab handle, nobody taking notice of her glazed, half-closed eyes. Half an hour later, she was at the Seoul

Express Bus Terminal, waiting for an intercity bus, still in the dissociative condition. And not long after that, she was standing in the back of a bus that was leaving Seoul behind.

Hungry Gal and Driver Park entered the media room at the clubhouse, and were met with a chilly reception. The various monitors and screens in the room were already set to pick up every possible report of a fire, including police and fire department radio chatter.

"How could you lose her?" said PJ, giving voice to what the Poet and ADMIN were silently wondering.

"It just happened, okay?" Hungry Gal was not in the mood for explaining herself.

Driver Park, for her part, seemed embarrassed to have let this occur on her watch.

The intercity bus coursed along a main highway across the countryside, passing forest brush, more distant trees, an even more distant mountain. Suddenly, everybody aboard heard the startling sound of an insistent pounding: next to her seat, Windy had found and extracted the emergency hammer designed for breaking the window in the event of an emergency, and was, in fact, breaking the window.

The bus driver immediately drove over to the side of the road, turned and shouted toward the back, "What is the nature of the emergency?" Only to see Windy, hammer in hand, moving towards him and the front door. When she got there, he immediately opened it for her and she exited the bus.

"Miss! What's wrong!?" he shouted after her. But he got no answer.

Windy dropped the hammer and continued sleepwalking away from the bus toward the trees. There was no access road or even trail, she just walked across the rough ground.

The bus driver had exited as well, and continued to call out, "Miss! Miss!" He considered running after her, but his passengers were shouting in confusion and now anger—he could not abandon the bus to chase after this apparently irrational young woman.

So he got back into his vehicle and called in a passenger incident report. As he watched Windy head into the trees and out of sight, he suddenly noticed in the far distance beyond her, a thin tendril of smoke.

The arson investigation trio pored over files and photos and maps, looking for some advance hint of where the next blaze would be set.

Suddenly, First Assistant Choi responded to something she had just heard over the radio channel via her earbuds. "Chief!" He glanced up. "Fire reported! Cheongpyeong National Forest!"

Investigator Kim wheeled his chair over to the big map on the wall. Choi made a mark at the location which was forty kilometers to the east of Seoul: completing the south-north; west-east locations with the details predicted by Kim.

"'East. Wood. Blue,' is what you said. Two out of three!" exclaimed Second Assistant Cho, amazed.

"Those are pine trees," said Choi, searching the internet for more details. "*Pinus koraiensis* in Latin. English translation: blue pine."

"Three's a charm," said Investigator Kim in heavily accented English.

"An intercity bus driver reported an incident enroute from Seoul Terminal to Gapyeong City," said First Assistant Choi, relaying what she had just heard over her earbuds. "A passenger stopped the bus and exited…"

She quickly located a spot on the map. "Here." The location was clearly within access of the national forest. "A young woman. She disappeared into the trees."

"Arsonist?" asked Second Assistant Cho.

"That doesn't make sense," said Kim. "They're operating as a team. And you don't take a bus to commit arson."

"Bus driver reported seeing smoke at the same time he reported the girl!" added Choi as more details came in.

"The fire must have just been set," said Cho. "That was the first report. Smoke. No visible flames."

"Seoul Bus Terminal to that location is an hour transit time," calculated Choi. They all considered these curious and seemingly contradictory bits of evidence.

"So she knew where the fire was *going* to be. An hour before it started. And she got on a bus to go see it."

Both assistants asked at once: "How?" "Why?"

There was no way to answer. They all mobilized to action, grabbed backpacks of equipment and headed for the door.

Every screen that Club H was watching had a news report about the Cheongpyeong forest fire. ADMIN called the Kid to inform him as they all went down to the limo. The boy was still at his folks' place in Ilsan, but had also seen the news. He seemed relieved to have an excuse to leave the encouraging but overbearing support from his family.

"Be the best Haetae ever!" said his mom.

"*Fighting*!" said his dad.

"Thanks Mom, thanks, Dad." He called a taxi but looking at the map on his phone he knew he'd never make it in time to help.

Windy saw herself striding across the emerald-colored landscape of the mythological world, past the table-like megaliths, along a winding stream, toward a distant glow. Suddenly, the glow exploded: like a small volcano had just erupted, sending sparks and flame shooting into the air.

Windy walked at the same pace across the actual forest she had exited the bus to enter. Before her, in the corresponding location to the inner volcano, was a sparking, flaming stand of pine trees: the real fire. It looked deadly. And to head straight into it seemed like death guaranteed.

A line of firefighting vehicles with sirens blasting and beacon lights flashing headed from Seoul toward the fire, to assist the locals.

The last vehicle in line was the van of the arson investigation team, with its own emergency beacons flashing. Second Assistant Cho drove, First Assistant Choi was in the passenger seat, Investigator Kim sat in the back.

Cho glanced in the rearview mirror outside his window. An object was approaching so fast from behind that the only thing he saw was a black blur. "Wow!" The van momentarily rocked with displaced air as the vehicle passed by only centimeters away. "They gotta be doing 250 kilometers per hour!"

Kim just watched it vanish in front of them.

The black blur was, of course, the Beast, flashing past the line of emergency vehicles at racing-car speeds.

Driver Park held onto the steering wheel with extreme concentration, like a Formula 1 competitor. ADMIN, Poet, PJ, and Hungry Gal were along for the ride, expressions tight, trying their best to pretend like this was just an everyday sort of drive in the countryside.

As Windy continued toward the blaze, the inner landscape was superimposed over the outer: mythological world and physical world overlapping. The closer she got to the coinciding images of erupting ground/forest fire, the louder became the sound of movement at her side. And a low, lionlike rumbling vocalization. She glanced towards the source, and caught a glimpse of a Haetae immediately to her left. Her own breath sped up with both anticipation and excitement. Then there was another: running at her right side. And another: right behind her. She tried to keep her gaze focused forward, at the burning ground/trees ahead of her.

A Haetae was there too. Moving in front of her, leading the way. She was surrounded by the creatures, as if in the midst of charging rhinos.

As if she was one of them.

Then the monster before her moved aside, to let her take the lead.

"How considerate was that?! It felt like an invitation to freedom. But as I didn't trust anything, including whether or not the sun would come up tomorrow morning, how could I trust becoming a monster? Even for just a few moments? Even if it was the only way to save my own life? That thought was enough to wake me up."

She shouted aloud as she had once before, in apology to the entire pack: "Next time for sure!"

Which completely jolted her out of the sleepwalking/fugue state. All trace of the mythological realm vanished. And so did the Haetae.

She was alone. Alone in the middle of a forest on fire, with maybe seconds to live.

"Wait! Come back! *Shit.*"

Walls of raging flame towered on all sides of her. The sound that came from them seemed to change: as if knowing she was now alone, the fire cackled.

Every thought and emotion vanished in the midst of the awesome terror of the blaze.

Then another sound cut through even the roar of flames: the thunderous propeller chop from a tanker plane flying low overhead. Windy looked up. A huge, cloudlike bloom of brightly colored fire retardant was falling toward her. On impact, all became pink.

As a team of hotshot firefighters headed for the line of trees and the fire behind it, Windy strode into view, coming right toward them. She was completely covered in bright pink fire retardant. No longer sleepwalking, she appeared dazed but uninjured. The firefighters started shouting into radios and to each other: "A survivor!" "Medical assistance required!" "She looks okay!"

By the time Arson Investigator Kim and his team arrived in their van, the base camp was a place of great activity and confusion: firefighting trucks, a tent-covered command center, emergency vehicles, news media, firefighters preparing to go into the trees, teams returning exhausted from the ongoing battle. Kim got out and quickly took stock of the situation. Moments later he wheeled up to the local commander in charge here.

"Arson Investigation, Seoul," announced Kim with friendliness, offering his badge.

"Thanks for making the trip, Chief," said the harried commander. "Anything I can do for you?"

"I'd ask you the same question. We're at your service." It was a disarming exchange that cut through any possible territoriality.

The commander appreciated the attitude. "The fire's twenty percent contained. Gonna be a long night. But we'll get it under control." Then: "There's a survivor."

"Female? Twenties?" interrupted Kim. The local firefighter was surprised that he knew about this.

"She a suspect?"

"Person of interest. Wouldn't take it beyond that, at this stage of the game." Kim continued as if only casually interested. "Where's she now?"

"Paramedics took her to the nearest hospital. In Sudong-Myeong."

Windy's clothes had been rubbed clean of retardant, but the pink color remained. She was being examined by a handsome ER physician. "Minor smoke inhalation... and this rash on your arm looks like an allergy to the flame retardant that saved your life. Seems like a good trade-off." He checked the intake report on a clipboard. "You said you have family in Seoul. Just curious, what were you doing out here? On a hike?"

"I came to stop the fire." She said it without thinking. The doctor smiled, believing she had just tried to make light of the situation.

"You were gonna kick some dirt on it?" he joked back.

But Windy was still disoriented from the experience and not entirely in her right senses yet. "I was gonna eat it."

"Baby Sis!" Hungry Gal rushed into view, took Windy by the sleeve, then turned to the physician. "What do I have to sign?"

Arson Investigator Kim noticed the limo exiting the hospital grounds just as he was getting out of the van. He immediately flashed on the moment when a black shape zoomed past them at supercar speed.

"She's in that car," he said with certainty.

The two assistants were accustomed to his leaps of predictive logic. But the claim still caught them off guard.

"Should we follow?"

"You saw what that vehicle can do," said Kim, shaking his head no. He called a number on his cell. The voice that answered was the commander he had just spoken with at the base camp.

"Hey Chief, what do you got?"

"A favor to ask, Commander. This is way out of my jurisdictional league, so, please don't hesitate to say no..."

A short time later the favor had been granted. A police roadblock had been set up, stopping and checking all traffic heading into Seoul. That included the Beast. Driver Park had no choice but to lower her window on approach: there was no other way out. But her hands tensed up on the steering wheel, as if she might suddenly accelerate through the blockade or try something even more desperate.

"Good afternoon, Miss. Lower the rest of the windows please."

Five more police officers slowly converged on the vehicle. All the windows rolled down, revealing ADMIN, Hungry Gal, Poet, and PJ. The cops ordered everybody out. Then they opened the trunk: it was empty.

At that moment, a helicopter passed overhead, heading back to Seoul.

Windy was inside the chopper; her pilot was Kid Kee. He had diverted to the airfield that housed his helicopter when he knew he couldn't reach the clubhouse in time to go with the others to help.

"Are you even old enough to fly this thing?"

"Technically, no. But you'd be surprised what a pile of money can buy."

In all the excitement of her escape from scrutiny, Windy had forgotten that she was pissed off.

"Oh, I imagine it can buy a lot."

He reacted, realizing he had said too much.

"I ran into my father today," Windy continued, "and he told me some snotty kid gave him a backpack full of cash to move out of the apartment." Windy stared at him. "So that I would have no choice but to stay with you guys? Let me guess, it was for my own safety?"

The Kid glanced over at her.

"Keep your eyes on the road, please."

"Sorry," he faced forward again.

"I don't actually believe these things can stay in the air."

"They don't always."

"That's great."

"I didn't tell the others," he said with zero shame. "It was my money. I don't have any friends in the house. They're all too old. And I don't have a social life on the outside. You're closer to me in age. I thought we could be friends."

"I don't make friends."

"I sort of figured."

"So that was a bad idea."

They were in sight of Seoul and the spectacular image of the city from this vantage momentarily overwrote all other considerations.

"You gonna move out?" he finally asked.

"No."

"Good."

"Nearly thirty hours after it began, the Cheongpyeong Forest fire is ninety percent under control, with no reported fatalities. As of yet, the cause of the fire has not been announced..."

The members of Club H watched the news updates on their phones as they waited on the rooftop. Windy finally stepped into view, her hair still with a tinge of pink from the fire retardant. The Kid was right behind her. The greetings were muted all around.

"I'm just gonna go and lay down," said Windy, not taking a seat.

"Let's talk first?" asked ADMIN. "A debriefing. While your memory is still fresh. Sleep could erase crucial details."

Windy considered, remained on her feet. "Alright."

"So what's your excuse this time?" said Hungry Gal, without further ado. Everybody shot looks at her, but she didn't care.

"That's what you have to say to me?"

"You almost got yourself killed," Hungry Gal continued. "Again. And good thing there were no hikers in the area. Or a busload of kids on a school trip. Because maybe they'd be dead too."

It sounded like a slap in the face. But Windy wasn't buying it. Or not all of it, anyway.

"Good job looking after me. You probably had your nose too far in a bowl of ramen to be bothered." She turned away from the table. "I'm going to sleep." And left them.

"That was a brief debriefing," said the Kid.

"Good job," said PJ to Hungry Gal.

Poet got up to follow after her, but PJ stopped him. "I'll go."

Poet considered himself something of a Daoist and liked the idea of always going as water goes: when the way was blocked, plunge not ahead but go around. "Let her know she is loved here," he said unexpectedly, sitting back down.

PJ was taken aback. "Right."

"Go ahead, Hero," said Hungry Gal as he left them. ADMIN sighed wearily.

"What?" she badgered him.

"Sometimes..." he answered.

"Sometimes what?"

"Sometimes you let your issues get in the way of your basic humanity," said ADMIN.

"What issues? What humanity? Humanity sucks," was her reply. "Why do we even bother protecting this place?"

She indicated the skyline of Seoul with a wave of her hand. "It's not like anybody even knows what we do for them."

"See?" said the Kid. "Bad attitude."

"You jerks are all the same," said Hungry Gal.

ADMIN seemed fed up, his patience for once at an end. "You know where the door is. Use it whenever you want."

"Great idea." She took off.

Windy had gotten lost trying to find her way back to her room. She was frustrated and in tears when PJ caught up to her. In a completely unexpected moment, they went into each other's arms and kissed, catching them both off guard. A few moments later, they didn't know what to do.

"I'm sorry," said PJ quickly. "I didn't mean that."

"You didn't?"

"I mean I did. But I didn't mean to scare you."

"I'm not scared."

"Good."

"But let's not do that again."

"Okay, we won't."

"Today," Windy clarified.

"Okay."

"Let's make some tea or something."

"Okay."

An hour later they were still in the clubhouse library, a low fire burning in the fireplace, and they were still sipping tea.

PJ indicated the dying flames. "Afraid of fire? All of us got over it. Because there's nothing to be afraid of. What is 'fire,' exactly? Some natural phenomenon shit discovered by cavemen to cook meat. To keep them from freezing and from being eaten by wolves. Like, a million years ago. Now, we got electricity and guns. We keep fire around to barbecue pork belly and light cigarettes. Out of nostalgia. It's almost sad." This was clearly coming from his growing feelings for her. "But something to fear? No way."

"I'm not afraid of fire," said Windy. *Suddenly, she flashed back to her earliest memory: as an infant surrounded by the flames. And saw something that she had not remembered until that moment: she had smiled and laughed in the midst of the roaring blaze.* "I've never been afraid of fire."

"Then what's... the problem?"

Windy gave him a look. "Is this part of the debriefing?"

"Of course not."

The burning log suddenly collapsed in on itself, as the fire sputtered and got even lower.

"I want to go for a walk," she said.

"Sure. Let's go."

"By myself."

"Call me if you want me to meet you somewhere."

"I will."

Windy left the library. PJ, surrounded by books which were not his thing at all, suddenly felt awkward even being there.

Arson Investigator Kim and his team had driven straight from Cheongpyeong Forest to their office, to see how the latest data point fit into the gut hypothesis.

The forest fire had been added to the map, which clearly demonstrated that the four fires indeed corresponded to the four cardinal directions: south and north, west and east.

"We tracked space, now we've got enough data points to consider time." Kim used his stylus and tablet to shoot four dates onto the screen.

"The time between each fire is getting shorter," observed First Assistant Choi.

Second Assistant Cho shook his head. "But by random amounts—"

"I should cuff you on the back of the head," interrupted Investigator Kim. "Like in the movies."

"You won't do that, Chief."

"Why not?"

"Not your style, sir."

"Too much bother, more like." He indicated the dates of the fires. "Seems random on first glance. But plot those times along a couple axes..." He tapped the stylus and suddenly the screen displayed the four dates on a graph. Then he drew a line connecting them: it looked like the turning of a snail shell.

"A curve," said Cho.

"A spiral, to be exact," answered his superior. "The same inward-rotating path that a mudang dances as she summons whatever deity she has promised her client. Right before the spirit descends to her, in the center of the ritual space, the middle of the gut." He overlaid the spiral across the map: it led to the center of the city.

"They set fires in the south, west, north, and east. What's left?" he asked rhetorically. "The center," said both of his staff at once.

As they worked their computers to bring up maps and possible targets, Kim filled in the rest. "Variables to look for... location: center; element: earth; color: yellow; time: tomorrow."

Deep underground, in the center of the spiral that had just been mapped in the office of Arson Investigation, Firestarter and his two men—in full protective gear, including welding masks—used a welding torch to make deep cuts into a thick piece of metal. The sparks flew in the darkness around them. They were prepping the next fire.

Or if the gut theory was correct: the final fire.

Hungry Gal Noh's family home was a penthouse apartment high above the Han River adjacent to the Ichon-dong neighborhood of Seoul. She had been given a pair of high-powered binoculars when she was a young girl, powerful enough to see the families gathering for picnics along the river, but not powerful enough to see if they were happy or not. She guessed, if her own family was anything to go on, that they were not.

She sat at one end of a long table set for a fancy Korean-Western fusion-style meal. Her mother sat at the other end. Servers brought out a multitude of side dishes made by the chef on staff and arranged them on the table.

"How's the apartment?" her mother asked, trying to be interested.

"I haven't lived there for five years," answered Hungry Gal. "I rent it out now."

Her mother, glancing up from her smartphone, had heard but not actually perceived the response. "Oh?"

"The people I rent it to sold all your furniture," Hungry Gal exaggerated, just to see if that would get a response.

"What people?" Again, the inquiry had no interest behind it.

"There's about ten of them. I don't keep count."

"Your father sends his regards."

"Is that him you're texting?

"Of course not."

"Then how do you know?"

"How do I know *what*?"

"That he sends his regards."

"I'm *guessing* he would. If he knew you were here."

The servers finished bringing out the side dishes, and now were bringing the main course: salmon bulgogi.

"Bon appétit," said her mother.

Hungry Gal considered the vast spread of food.

"I'm not hungry."

Windy had walked a good distance away. Her thoughtful and just a little bit worried expression made it clear this was no fugue-state journey but, just as she had told PJ, only a walk. The street was one of many narrow pathways along the side of this series of hills. The lights of the city were spread out before her. It was very pretty. But also seemed lonely to her now.

She turned to look for the mansion, still a bit unfamiliar with the neighborhood. Then she saw a lovely glow in the distance: a traditional Korean oil lamp set in a window of the clubhouse. The soft flicker from the single flame was encouraging and welcoming. Windy couldn't help but smile. And headed back toward her new home.

Windy located and opened a door on the inside that seemed to correspond to the window she had seen on the outside. She found herself in a space she had not seen before: a small, pretty reading room that looked like it would have been appropriate in the home of a late nineteenth-century Korean poet. Walls were lined with books, there was a writing desk, a couple of spare chairs. And an antique oil lamp, flame flickering, in the window where Poet had put it. For her.

She was surprised to see him. She had expected it would be PJ. But she didn't mind at all.

"I didn't even know this room was here…"

"The lamp told you." He was at the writing desk, using an old fountain pen on paper.

"Yeah. I guess it did." She watched him for a moment. "I'm surprised you could even light it."

"This lamp and I have known each other for years. It trusts that I won't just snuff the flame out arbitrarily." He smiled. "Though there is always that chance."

"What are you writing?"

"A letter to my grandmother."

"That's great. I wish I knew my grandmother."

"You can borrow mine."

Windy stepped further into the room, taking in the pretty surroundings, and finally, unable to keep herself from doing so, gazed at the lamp, moving close to it.

Poet watched her for a moment.

"Look. Your slightest breath makes the flame tremble. It's afraid of you." He indicated the window. "And yet, it called you here. Because that's what an old lamp, placed in a window, has always done. It says: 'Come home.' It has always said: 'Come home.' Every lamp, placed in every window. By every person who sat waiting. For every person who wandered."

"Come home," she repeated. They were both quiet for a moment.

"You don't trust people. And you don't trust them." He indicated a painting of a Haetae on the wall. "I know you were betrayed, once."

"Do you really?" she bristled.

He shrugged. "The biographical details are known. You're a member of this Club, after all. And I can reasonably guess at your emotional response to that formative trauma."

She was satisfied by the response. "Once is enough. For a lifetime."

"But if you don't trust, you can't love. Betrayal makes love possible."

"That doesn't make sense."

"If the possibility of being hurt, of being disappointed, doesn't exist, then what kind of bond is that? It's not love."

"Did you learn that the hard way?"

He indicated the rows of volumes on the wall. "Read it in a book."

"Of course you did," she said, not hiding her sarcasm.

Despite the protective armor of that cynicism, Windy suddenly needed to change the subject. She indicated a small marble ink stamp on the desk of the fire-eating creature. "They're so darn cute."

"Yes. They are," he agreed. "Ugly-Cute."

"Or Cute-Ugly." She smiled.

He finished the letter to his grandmother, folded the page. "I've got to send this." Then he stood away from the desk and moved to the lamp. And burned the letter over the open flame.

Windy realized that his grandmother was dead.

"I'm sorry," she said.

"I try to keep in touch." But there was a sadness on his face. They both watched the lone flame ignite the letter, which quickly became smoke and ashes, vanishing in the air, like a paper prayer burned at a funeral.

The following morning, at the offices of the Seoul Metropolitan Police Agency in Gwanghwamun, Arson Investigator Kim had covered the whiteboard of the conference room they had given him with the same variables and hypotheticals that stretched across the one at his office: the map with the last four fires in allegedly shamanistic formation, forensic sketch artist drawings of the two suspects driving the fuel tanker truck, and a still image taken from a TV news video that showed Windy covered in pink fire retardant just after she was rescued from the burning forest.

Kim had wheeled himself back and forth in front of it for his briefing, which he had just finished. "Questions?" he asked.

The dozen officers who had been assembled to watch this discussion all look baffled.

The police captain finally spoke up. "A gut you say?"

Kim nodded. "The mind of an arsonist has an active obsessional component. You never know what you'll find when the evidence gives you a glimpse inside."

Nobody responded. They shifted in their seats, checked cell phones, glanced at their captain as if to say, what is this shit?

The captain could only extend courtesy to a fellow professional for just so long—he was a busy man. "Thank you, Chief. We'll take over from here."

Investigator Kim knew he wouldn't be getting any further cooperation or guarantees of assistance than that. "Captain. Officers. Thank you for your time."

One of the cops started clapping as if at the theater. A look from the captain shut him down. After Kim and his team exited the door, the captain gave the whiteboard a last glance, while his officers stood up to go back to work. He indicated the endpoint of the spiraling arson locations: the center of the city.

"Tell Traffic to keep an eye open for anything fire-buggy

in the city center... while they're issuing parking tickets." Then he waved at the renderings of the two arsonists and the photo of Windy covered in pink. "And run some facial recognition on the two suspects and the person of interest."

There was grumbling from the cops who clearly thought this had been a complete waste of time. The captain turned and faced them. "It's the least we can do."

Then the attendees started inexplicably laughing. He looked over his shoulder and saw that one of his officers with an artistic bent was rapid sketching a bunch of frantic circles and arrows and exclamation points in accomplished calligraphic style. As if to emphasize the obsessive nature of the arson investigator himself.

The captain considered the man's artistry—"Not bad"—but cuffed him on the side of the head regardless. "Show some respect for a fellow law enforcement officer, you little shit."

In the corridor just outside the conference room, Kim's assistants looked disappointed by the lack of enthusiasm on the part of the police. He picked up on that mood, as he picked up on everything. "Speak your truth and let God sort it out."

"Which god?" suddenly blurted Second Assistant Cho, who seemed to have something on his mind.

"What?"

"Which god are the arsonists trying to summon?"

"We live in a godless universe," came the answer from his boss, "and that being the case, it doesn't matter who they think they are summoning. Nobody is going to answer."

Cho wouldn't back down, not this time. "But it's obviously important to them. Or they wouldn't be going through all this trouble."

"Which makes it worth our considering," said Kim, as he quickly took the notion to its natural conclusion. "As the identification of who or what they think they are bringing into this world could be an indication as to who they are."

Second Assistant looked proud. Finally, he got one.

Windy woke up in the reading room where she had fallen asleep in a chair after she and Poet had talked long enough into the night for the oil lamp to burn down and out. She had dreamt of sleeping in a pack or a pride or a pod: of wolves, lions, allosaurs. The ultimate safety net. Nothing could harm her. It would have to get through everybody else to get to her, and since everybody by definition would die for everybody else, that could never happen.

The morning sun shone through the window; one glance around told her she was alone. There was no obvious reason to be alarmed at Poet's absence. He had no doubt gone to his own room after Windy dozed off. But something told her that one of the pack or pride or pod had gone missing.

In the clubhouse underground gym, ADMIN shot baskets while the Kid pulled himself up a climbing wall.

"You know what I think?" the boy said, dangling from one hand.

"That I can't sink this three-pointer."

"That too."

ADMIN took the very long shot, which swished next to the basket without touching anything.

"I think they're trying to catch one of us," continued the Kid.

ADMIN nodded. "It's possible or even likely that Windy has been identified as a person of interest by the Arson Investigation Department. But as she has broken no laws, that investigation won't go anywhere."

"I mean the arsonists. The arsonists are trying to catch one of us."

ADMIN reacted. That hadn't occurred to him. "Continue the thought."

"Zero apparent connection between four different fires: no casualties, no hostages, no statement of demands, no political manifesto, not even a common method of ignition. In fact, there's only one thing in common, to all them."

"Us."

"Us."

ADMIN just looked at him. The basketball continued to bounce: up and down, up and down.

Then his phone buzzed and he answered it. Driver Park had called to let him know what had happened. She was at the wheel of the Beast, Windy rode in back. Visible through the windshield, half a block in front of them, was Poet, sleepwalking to the next fire.

"Stay with him as close as possible," said ADMIN, "even if you have to enter the blaze yourselves. He may be in danger."

As Driver Park ended the call, Windy suddenly was alarmed. "Where did he go?"

Park blinked and stared out the windshield, astonished.

Poet had simply vanished. As if the earth had swallowed him up.

Which was exactly what had happened.

PJ was in the middle of a Yudo sparring bout at the local dojo he belonged to, as nobody in the clubhouse shared his enthusiasm for fighting. His phone sat in his locker with his street clothes. It buzzed insistently, but at that moment he had thrown his opponent to the mat and gone right into a hold, which had quickly been broken. He was again on his feet and maneuvering for a throw. The part of his brain that might have given PJ his own intuitive warning that something was up with one of his fellow club members was overwhelmed by the intense physical activity, like the flame of a candle in the light of the noonday sun. And so the bout continued, and so the warning inside his head went unheeded.

Hungry Gal stood in front of her parents' refrigerators, plural: three of them were lined up against the wide and bare kitchen wall, as if waiting to be shot. She had opened all the doors and was staring at the food opportunities inside. Anywhere else, and the contents would have sent

her salivary glands into overdrive, but here, at "home,"
everything tasted like ashes in her mouth. So she almost
welcomed the Kakao text that arrived without warning
from the Club H administrator, with its attached file that
when opened, revealed a map of the neighborhood of
Sinseol-dong: Poet's last known location. She closed the
app. Considered again the inner landscape of the massive
appliances before her and deciding it was not going to get
any better anytime soon, answered the call to duty.

Poet had climbed down a metal access ladder into the
deep darkness below. A tiny spot of light far overhead
indicated the street above that he had just left behind. In
his fugue state, the lack of light didn't seem to matter, as
he followed a different kind of reckoning than that of the
sunlit world above.

Firestarter Kan's face was lit by a tiny pool of light
in the otherwise completely dark surroundings. His two
accomplices stood near, using their cell phones as light
sources so he could see what he was doing: hitting the
power button of a small, electronic activator.

~~~

Windy and Driver Park searched the streets for Poet, finding nothing that told them how he might have disappeared. Suddenly, there was a distant rumble below their feet and a slight shaking like a minor temblor. Locals and passersby took notice but brushed it off, as Seoul was not accustomed to earthquakes. Windy and the limo driver, suspecting the worse, glanced around and spotted a manhole cover. Windy rushed toward it, but Driver Park grabbed her sleeve to stop her, just as: boom! The cover flew upward, propelled by air pressure from an explosion below. It spun in the air like a flipped coin, over and over. Then a succession of manhole covers did the same: boom! boom! boom! People screamed and shouted and took cover as the heavy metal discs finally landed with a clanging smash on the ground and through a few rooftops.

The traffic officer who had just printed out a parking citation for the Beast—which had been parked illegally, as usual—and stuck it onto the windshield, ducked when she heard the explosions and saw the columns of smoke up the street, each white, billowing pillar corresponding to the blown manhole covers. Emergency alarms blared, there were shouts and screams and confusion. "Dispatch, Traffic Patrol," she called in her report. "I was told to watch for anything unusual…"

The space beneath the streets was an underworld of mythic ingredients: a maze of subterranean tunnels, running creeks, broken vaults, wall surfaces of every kind of material—concrete and metal, ceramic and stone—from every era of the city, going back centuries. Small fires were scattered everywhere, contributing an infernal, Dantean illumination. Poet headed deeper and deeper into this hellish environment with the same combination of expressionless face and directional intention that always seemed to accompany the fugue state.

Windy and Driver Park climbed down the same kind of ladder Poet had used to access the world below. But heavy fumes rose to greet them. They started coughing and their eyes burned and they had no alternative but to climb back up toward the street, and leave Poet to whatever it was he would encounter beneath their feet.

"Dongdaemun district, Sinseol neighborhood," said First Assistant Choi, locating the site of the latest report on the Arson Investigation unit's big board. "The central end of the spiral, just like you said, sir."

"Point of origin?" asked Arson Investigator Kim.

"Unspecified. Smoke and gasses reported from the manhole covers and sewer openings," continued Choi.

"Earth!" interrupted Second Assistant Cho. He was reading from the "variables to look for" list they had made for predicting the next fire.

"Underground," nodded Kim. "Sounds like 'earth' to me."

"No casualty reports," said First Assistant Choi. "No alarms from the metro system. So where underground...?"

"Color: yellow," stated the arson investigator, off the same list of variables.

Second Assistant Cho rushed to his computer, pulling up street photos of the area. "Maybe there's a building that color..."

Kim had wheeled himself over to a filing cabinet and was pulling city blueprints out of an old file. "Yellow... yellow..." He found what he was looking for, unfolding an old blueprint for their inspection that looked to be from decades ago. "The first attempt at a subway system left a ghost station right here." He indicated a location far below a street in the Sinseol area. "Abandoned in 1961. Ten years before Seoul had a successful Metro."

Cho read the blueprint. "Yellow Line."

In the basement archive of the Club H mansion, after tearing through a pile of books and old documents, ADMIN and the Kid had located their own copy of the very same blueprint Arson Investigator Kim had found. And they stared at the very same "ghost station" far below the surface of the street. ADMIN quickly scanned the blueprint with his phone and uploaded it to the rest of the crew.

At the location itself, smoke billowed up from below, fire trucks and police cars rushed to the scene, sirens wailed, alarms blared, lights flashed, and the news coverage was scant on details. "Columns of smoke and shaking streets, but authorities have yet to determine the cause…"

Ghost station. The point of origin of the fire: the eerie, deserted space of an abandoned subway station. Rider landing, support columns, signs, tracks, there was even an old subway car. Flames were everywhere. And Poet was sleepwalking right into it.

But Poet literally only half saw those images—*the legendary world accessed by his fugue state was already superimposed over the real one: the dolmens, the green hills, the Haetae that gathered around him as he moved.*

Firestarter and his two helpers stared at Poet as he approached from across the burning station. The Titanis CEO had been waiting for him here, had known or at least hoped he would come, for this had been the goal all along: the arsons had indeed been designed as a gigantic gut ritual, whose space was Seoul itself. But there was a catch: a medium was needed, more powerful than one that could be hired; it had to be a member of the otherwise secret Club H, which Firestarter's years of obsessive research had led him to.

"To see what those eyes have seen," he said as Poet approached. "And what those eyes *will* see..." But Poet's face was still blank; was he even aware of these guys?

Firestarter raised his voice. "Hail, Prometheus. Fire-bringer. You who stole the sacred flame from Olympus. From Zeus himself, King of the Gods..." Poet paused in his forward movement, as if the words of the invocation had penetrated his otherwise opaque state of awareness. His eyes reflected the fires around him, and seemed to react to the words shouted like a summons. "... and brought that gift to Earth!"

In Poet's inner gaze, the Neolithic Korean plain and the Haetae gathering around him seemed to dissolve away, replaced by a mist as of clouds, on a rocky mountainside. "A gift to human-kind," continued the voice from outside Poet's head. "Hail Prometheus. Your deliverer has come. He approaches even now."

A melancholic sigh came from nearby. Poet, walking across this Greek mythological landscape, turned toward the source of the sound: a rocky crag, swirled with clouds. The mist parted and Poet caught a glimpse of a handsome, powerfully built but exceedingly weary being: Prometheus, the Titan of Greek myth, chained to a rock.

The Titan saw Poet, as well. And for a moment, the sudden appearance of a visitor after millennia of solitary confinement made him smile. "What is it you want of me? Human being... You are, human, correct?"

"Yes," answered Poet, both still in a trance and simultaneously entranced by this sudden encounter with a clearly superior being. "I am human."

"They always wanted something," said Prometheus, almost to himself.

Poet's delicate awareness of this razor's edge state of conscious started slipping in and out of the fugue state, and he was aware both of Prometheus in the Greek mythological world and Firestarter in the burning underground metro station.

"What... did I just see...?" he asked aloud.

Firestarter excitedly leaned closer. "Or 'whom'...? Whom do you see?"

"A tall man... chained to a rock."

"Success. Incredible." Firestarter turned to his cronies. "We have bridged the universes." He turned back to Poet: "That is Prometheus. My friend, you are in the presence of the savior of humanity."

Poet repeated the name: "Prometheus."

And in the realm of Greek myth, the being responded: "Yes, that is what you people called me. A long time ago."

"Ask him for a gift," said Firestarter to Poet. "Tell him of our need."

Poet conveyed the request. "Is there a gift? For us?"

"If you break these chains. I will gift you indeed." The Titan held one of his chained hands palm up. A sphere materialized on it, filling his hand. It was covered in tiny gears and levers, like a globular version of the Antikythera mechanism, and it shimmered with cosmic power and beauty, as if the most perfect combination of technology and nature.

"Yes," reported Poet, in awe. "There is a gift." *The cloudy mist suddenly swirled around him, the image of the mountain blurred again for a moment, interpenetrated with the green and stone-strewn plain of the Haetae.*

"You must free him," directed Firestarter. "Break the chains."

The two henchmen were getting concerned about the

flames that had become stronger now and were moving closer and closer. There was no way out unless Poet saved them. And he appeared too distracted for that to happen.

"Sir," said Henchman #1, "we're cutting it close. We'll never get out on our own."

"Prometheus will preserve us," came the answer.

That wasn't good enough for Henchman #2, who turned and bolted but didn't get far until his he was hit by a fierce draft of flame that blew him out of their sight.

Henchman #1 steeled himself to stick it out with his boss.

"Break those chains!" insisted Firestarter, right into Poet's ear.

In Poet's vision, Prometheus and his rock flickered momentarily back into view. Poet's gaze focused on the chains that bound the Titan to the stone. He picked up a large rock and stepped closer, movements still unsure.

Prometheus smiled what seemed a genuinely compassionate smile and he indicated with a shake a link on one of the chains. "Strike here. There is a weak point. You only need disturb the bond for a moment. I will do the rest."

Poet closed the distance between them, then paused, momentarily overawed by the presence of this superior alien being.

"Don't be afraid," said Prometheus. "No harm will come to you."

Poet raised the rock to strike where the Titan indicated; suddenly, there was a terrifying shriek, and the huge eagle of Zeus plummeted out of the sky, driving its massive beak into the Titan's exposed torso. Prometheus screamed in agony.

Poet dropped the stone and watched in horrified fascination, unable to move, as if frozen in place in the middle of nightmare. The voice of Firestarter could barely be heard from the other world. "Break... the... chains..." Poet's face didn't register the command.

Then the clouds swirled again, taking Prometheus and his agony from view, suddenly replaced by the realm of the Haetae. The creature nearest to Poet gave him its famous smile—and Poet became one of them.

The ghost station was practically an inferno. Poet and Haetae were superimposed one over the other. Their mouths opened: there was a tremendous rushing roar and moaning/shrieking of flames. As the fire hurtled with impossible speed toward the open maw: as if pulled in by a black hole.

In a moment, the blaze was completely extinguished.

Poet woke from his fugue state. He barely registered the burned, dead bodies of Firestarter Kan and his remaining henchman. They had not been protected by

Prometheus as Kan had promised: their hoped-for savior and benefactor had been left bound to his rock and his torture.

Dazed, Poet stumbled away from the scene.

A short time later, firefighters pulled an instrument on a long cord up from a utility shaft that no longer had its manhole cover. Arson Investigator Kim watched with his assistants as one of the firefighters read with amazement the data off the instrument. "Temperature is... normal."

"There's enough fuel down there to keep a fire going for weeks," responded Kim, an uncharacteristic edge to his voice. "It cannot have gone out on its own."

Second Assistant Cho asked what was on everybody's mind. "Then who put it out?"

For once, the arson investigator's cool demeanor gave way to frustration: "Not 'who'—there is no 'who' that could have done this. No reason to personify the cause. 'How was a conflagration of this magnitude inexplicably extinguished?' is the question to ask. 'How,' not 'who.' " But his anger suppressed the growing doubts in his own mind. Who, indeed?

PJ rushed through a broken underground culvert, splashing through brackish water, looking for Poet. "Where are you, hyung? It's me. Where are you?"

Then he saw him in the trench ahead, crouched down waist deep in the water, disoriented, holding one hand up and open in a pantomime mimicry of what he had seen Prometheus do when the Titan had revealed the "gift."

PJ cautiously approached. "Hey, how are you doing?"

"Not sure."

"Want to go home?"

Poet looked at him for a moment. "I want to sleep."

"That can be arranged."

"But I don't think I can." His eyes were glassy, as if the momentous and disturbing experience in the other world was still trailing across his brain.

"You can."

In a matter of seconds, PJ had hauled Poet onto his back and was carrying him piggyback, chanting "Oh boo-bah, oh boo-bah..."

PJ emerged out of the culvert several minutes later still hauling Poet, who now was fast asleep. Windy, Driver Park, ADMIN, and the Kid were waiting. Hungry Gal suddenly stepped up to join them, making it the full crew. They converged on the pair the moment they saw them.

A massive tiger sat just outside a cave; the long, thin pipe he smoked extended far past the reach of his deadly claws, and so, naturally, a pair of helpful rabbits had packed and lit it for him.

"Hercules came out of the Underworld, Dante out of the Inferno, the Ginseng Warrior out of the Ogre's cave, and even Jesus himself spent a Saturday in Hell. But I didn't think of any of that. I just saw two boys coming up into the light of day, in the middle of Seoul. Two boys that I loved."

Poet Jun slept around clock for nearly two days, as his housemates kept vigil at his side in shifts, with Windy Lee and PJ Kwon doing the most time. He stirred and roused for just a few seconds every few hours or so, enough to demonstrate to the others that he was not in a coma and that it was best to keep him at home; rather that than risk he talk in his sleep in a hospital about what had happened at the ghost metro station in hearing range of doctor and nurses and attendants and anybody else who happened by: like a police officer or an arson investigator.

The fragrance from a big pot of seolleongtang that ADMIN Yoon had made finally woke him up. The beef bone soup revived his body and the presence of his comrades revived his spirits. He was eager to join them on the rooftop for a debriefing.

But he said that he remembered almost nothing of his encounter in the abandoned subway station. "I was with the Haetae the whole time. I don't know that I ever actually perceived the arsonists. You said there were two of them?"

"Two bodies were recovered," repeated ADMIN. "The police haven't released their identities."

"Probably not enough left of them to figure that out," ventured Kid Kee.

"Certainly not this quickly," agreed ADMIN.

"I wish I had more to tell you," said Poet. "I guess with their deaths, this is a 'case closed' sort of thing? And we can get on with our lives?"

"Such as they are," concluded Hungry Gal Noh.

The group was accustomed to openness with respect to their fire-eating experiences. Sharing that short of information counted as self-preservation. And so when something was left unsaid, they all felt it.

Windy had just discovered the clubhouse sauna, and had started to wonder if there actually was an end to the number of rooms the mansion-sized hanok seemed to have. Driver Park was already there with a towel over her head, taking in the heat and steam, when Windy entered, wrapped in a towel, and sat down across from her.

The limo driver had never warmed to her, and vice versa. So Windy was taken aback when the woman spoke first. "How is he?"

"Poet? I don't know."

Driver Park raised an eyebrow. "Why not?"

"I can't find him."

"Really."

A few awkward moments passed. Awkward for Windy, at any rate. The driver didn't seem to care.

"Maybe he went to visit his grandmother's grave," said Windy, guessing.

"He never knew his grandmother."

"But I thought—"

"He's an orphan. Like you."

"I'm half an orphan."

"Our Poet grew up in an orphanage."

Windy was taken aback, even disturbed by that information. "He never said—"

"He has his reasons."

Windy considered for a moment. "So maybe he went to visit the orphanage."

"Or what's left of it."

Windy found Poet just outside Seoul, at what was left of an orphanage that had burned down more than twenty years before. He had made two small mounds of dirt and placed a stick of incense on top of them. But every time he tried to light a match to light the incense, it went out.

"My ceramics instructor complained that he couldn't keep the kiln lit when I was around." Windy stepped into view.

Poet smiled. "Comes with our territory."

Windy considered the charred ruins of the buildings around them. "What happened here?"

"There was a fire."

"There always is."

"Yes. It seems that way, doesn't it?" He went back in memory. "I was ten. The shouting woke me up. There was smoke everywhere. They yelled at everybody to get outside, but I stopped halfway. It was the first time that I experienced the Haetae."

"You put out the fire?" Windy wondered, as the broken walls and blackened bricks scattered around them suggested that the blaze had done a complete job.

"Yes. But apparently, I had a couple of scores to settle first."

"What do you mean?"

"The director of the orphanage and one of the head teachers were still inside the building. Everybody else had gotten out. I saw the Haetae, I instinctively knew that they would consume the flames. But I waited. I didn't let them in. Didn't let one of them come through. Until those two people were dead."

Windy was taken aback by the admission. "Did they... do something to you?"

"Hurt me? I don't remember that."

"I searched on Haetae after I met you guys. They don't just extinguish fires. It said our ancestors believed they could tell right from wrong, and could punish the evil and the corrupt. Maybe you repressed what was done to you. But the Haetae knew."

"I've considered it," said Poet, trying one last time to light the incense. "But I think I just didn't like them. Like kids sometimes don't. So at ten years old, I was judge, jury, and executioner of two people who didn't deserve to die." He gave up on the incense, turned to her. "I need to atone for that... sin. Do something to make up for it."

"But every time you end a fire, you save people's lives."

"Something more."

"Like what?"

He smiled. But didn't answer. "Let's go see a play."

"Now? What play?"

"Yes or no."

Windy looked at him for a moment. Her autonomic inability to trust kicked in like getting hit by a reflex hammer. But how much trust was needed for some stupid play?

"Okay."

They touched down in Athens, Greece after a twelve-hour flight, took a two-hour taxi ride that skirted the huge city of Athens itself, and left the peninsula of Attica behind for that of Peloponnesus to the west, coursing along a narrow road that wound through rocky hills dotted with sparse pockets of brush and low gnarled trees. The cloud cover shifted mercurially, blocking then revealing the bright sunlight from moment to moment: the shadows below seemed to dance with each other—or maybe they were fighting like hoplites.

Poet glimpsed something off the side of the road and asked the taxi driver to pull over and stop. Windy went with him, mystified, as he walked several meters across the tall grass to what he had seen from the car: a plain, quadrangular column of stone, chest high. It was a herm, he explained: an ancient sculpture dedicated to Hermes, the Greek god of travel and borders among other appellations. The head was missing and so were the genitals, which left nothing distinguishable: no doubt the only reason the monument was still standing there after more than two thousand years, rather than in some museum basement or somebody's garden.

Poet plucked a flower from one of the tall grasses, quickly fashioned it into a loop, and crowned the broken stone. "Greetings, Hermes. Guard our journeys and let your luck go with us, no matter where we find ourselves."

He turned and headed back to the waiting taxi.

"What was that about?" asked Windy.

"When in Rome, do as the Romans do," Poet quoted the old saying.

"We're in Greece."

They arrived at their destination less than an hour later, just as the sun was going down: the Ancient Theater of Epidaurus. *Prometheus Bound*, written by Aeschylus, the most famous playwright in ancient Greece, was being performed that evening: a nearly 2500-year-old play in a nearly 2500-year-old theater. The amphitheater was completely without cover and exposed to the sky, constructed of stone, perfectly situated in a natural bowl in the landscape, with the audience looking down toward the stage.

Windy and Poet moved to their seats among the packed visitors, placed the earbuds provided by the theater staff as they went, and activated the simultaneous interpretation into Korean: "The play retells the myth of Prometheus, a Titan who stole fire from Zeus, ruler of Olympus, and gave it to humans, who had struggled for endless millennia in darkness, in the cold, and in their own ignorance." They sat down on bare rock. "The tale opens with the forging of the chains that will bind Prometheus to a rock as punishment for his offense against the gods..." The lights went down in the audience, and came up on the stage. "And for his love of humanity..."

On the stage below, the actor playing Hephaestus, blacksmith to the gods, banged on a piece of chain with hammer and anvil, complaining about his boss, the chief of the deities of Olympus. "The mind of Zeus is unknowable. But he has newly achieved his throne, and like all freshly forged kings, his policies are brutal..."

Windy couldn't help but glance from stage to sky: the setting was almost unreal, and she could barely keep herself from dreaming right where they sat. Eventually, the main character was revealed below: Prometheus, portrayed by an actor being chained to a simple wooden scaffolding that represented the side of a mountain. "See what has been done to me!" he cried out. "I am to be tormented for endless years! Bound to this wretchedness because I took pity on the mortals! I stole for them the fire of Heaven!"

Windy glanced at Poet, smiled to see that he too, seemed entranced by the surroundings and the play itself: his eyes were shining.

But she did not see what his eyes saw: the Greek mythological landscape superimposed over this one. Poet climbed the same peak he had ascended when he met the god/alien/being-from-an-alternate-universe that he had encountered during the fugue state at the ghost metro station under the streets of Seoul.

Prometheus was alone at his rock, a madness in his eyes. Then he saw Poet and the madness vanished. He smiled. "Again, you have come to pay me a visit."

"Yes."

"You are able to travel between the realms."

"Not at will," explained Poet. "I'm summoned by mythical creatures of my own culture. I function as a conduit for them."

"Mythical." Prometheus laughed brightly. Then he considered the astonishing implications of Poet's words. "You bring them into your own world, and they take action there?"

"Yes."

"That is a good trick."

"For only a few moments. For them to do what they want to do."

"And what do they want to do?"

"Eat fire."

Prometheus smiled. "The irony of it."

"I must agree."

Poet explained that he had used the stage play being performed at Epidaurus as a way to induce the altered state of consciousness he needed to bridge the gap between their two realities. As there was no fire that had called him into action, and so no other route that he could take to reach the mythical realm.

"But I am the very essence of fire," responded the being chained to the peak.

"That's a metaphor, isn't it?" asked Poet.

"True enough. I did not gift your ancestors with literal flames. I showed them how to use fire to turn stone ore into metal. For that, my freedom was taken *from me, as you see."* He lifted his chains. *"There are those of my kind who do not wish us to share knowledge with more... primitive creatures, please excuse the term."*

"I wouldn't deny it."

"So you have returned to free me?" Prometheus tried to keep the hope out of his voice.

"You promised a gift."

"If you break my bonds? Yes." Again, the orrery-like mechanism appeared on his palm. And again, its appearance made Poet almost dizzy.

"What does it do?"

"Turns light into matter," the Titan said simply. "On a macroscopic—indeed, grand—scale. Every advanced species must come to this knowledge sooner or later. Or it dies."

Poet realized that such a process would be a technological leap forward as great as the one that had left the Stone Age behind.

"Free me," Prometheus pleaded. "And this gift is yours."

"I have no way of carrying it into my world."

"You said you were a conduit—"

"It's beyond my ability." Poet smiled. "But I know someone who can. Probably."

"Probably?" There was a flash of titanic fury on the

demigod's face, quickly suppressed. And again, he seemed supernally empathetic. The cry of the approaching eagle that was his daily torture interrupted the exchange between them.

"Please hurry," said Prometheus.

Windy realized that her cell phone was vibrating. She checked her Kakao app to see that PJ had just texted her: "Where?!" Windy glanced at Poet, who seemed to have nodded off, took a quick selfie with him in frame, then uploaded it to PJ.

When PJ saw her text of "Epidaurus! Greece!" and the pic, he was amazed and disconcerted and jealous. He sent her a Kakao friend gif of Ryan unhappily knocking over a couple of LEGO-style stacked towers in response, then quickly did a NAVER search on his phone for "Epidaurus." The first thing that popped up was the ancient theater and the schedule of performance's including tonight's *Prometheus Bound*. He did another search, this time on the name "Prometheus"—and dozens of old European master paintings appeared: dramatic and sometimes violent depictions over the centuries of the Titan chained to the rock. PJ started to read...

Poet stirred next to her, and seemed to wake up from a nap. He took Windy's hand and she didn't take it back. Windy continued to watch the play, captivated not just by the production, but by the surroundings.

A chorus of performers had gathered near the actor playing the enchained Titan. "We see, Prometheus! A mist of tears rushes to our eyes! To find you left here, bound to this rock, for all time!" In response, the character of Prometheus cried out in agony.

When it was all over, Windy and Poet kept still on the limestone bench. Until everybody left and they were alone. The ancient stones, the countless stars overhead, the lulling chirrup of cicadas that was the only sound they heard: it was all so entrancing they just could not leave. Windy rested her head on his shoulder. And they stayed like that until the taxicab arrived like a chariot from another world.

Sol appeared over the horizon the way it only can at ten thousand meters above the ground. Windy woke to find Poet staring out the window at the dawn. "From here, the sun looks like the flame of a candle."

She too stared out the window. He was right: it looked small and perfect, like a tiny piece of fire.

Driver Park met them at Incheon and drove them back to the clubhouse. Along the way, she couldn't help but notice in the rearview mirror that Windy and Poet rested with heads touching together. For once, the driver's expression revealed her emotions: she wasn't happy about this development. But whether her affections were with Poet or with the new girl was not certain. Not even to her.

Windy woke the next day, shook off her jetlag and looked for Poet, checking the clubroom, the library, the gym, the sauna, even the ancient ring of stones in the subterranean chamber. But he was nowhere to be found.

Windy stuck her head into the kitchen, saw Hungry Gal working a professional level espresso machine. "Have you seen—"

"No," answered Hungry Gal, without waiting for a name. News had apparently gotten around.

Windy stepped out the front door and was surprised to find PJ standing there. Having a cigarette. "I didn't think any of us smoked."

"A fire-eater who smokes. Yeah, seems a bit

counterintuitive." He put out the cigarette. "You doing anything?"

Windy was still disappointed at not finding Poet anywhere and not hearing from him. "I guess not."

They took a taxi halfway up the side of Namsan Mountain and rode the cable car the rest of the way to the popular mountaintop park that featured views of the entire city, Namsan Tower, lots of visitors, a big yellow Haetae statue known as "haechi" that was the official mascot of Seoul, and, of course, the chain link fences filled with love locks—small, heart-shaped padlocks attached by hopeful couples who had written their names across them in felt tip pen.

An ajusshi was seated on a bench with a heavy set of bolt cutters across his lap and a handwritten sign around his neck that read: "I break hearts: 10,000 won."

"That is the best business concept I've ever seen." PJ was thrilled by the sight. "Ajusshi! Ajusshi!" He tugged Windy toward the older man.

A very short time later, PJ had located a padlock on one of the fences that read "PJ + Peggy" and Windy watched bemused as the man with the bolt cutter grabbed onto the shackle of the lock.

"Cheap at half the price," PJ declared, as—kerchunk—the lock snapped apart. The man turned away, but PJ grabbed his sleeve. "We're just getting started." Kerchunk! Three more "PJ + X" love locks were broken apart by the ajusshi's bolt cutters.

Windy considered the shattered hearts as PJ gathered up the pieces and tossed them into a trash bin. "You're a busy guy."

"Not really, but it accumulates over the years."

A leisurely stroll put them at one of the lookout points, staring north toward the massively tall superstructure of the building under construction in Jongno. PJ was impressed. "Wow. The Tower of Olympus. Never seen it from this high."

They both stared for a few moments at the impressive piece of engineering and construction—still an open and bare superstructure of steel beams and concrete.

"So how was Greece," he finally asked.

"Amazing."

"The play?"

"Everything."

"I'm trying not to sound jealous," he confessed, as though it wasn't obvious.

"Thank you," said Windy unexpectedly.

"For what."

"For making me feel... I don't know. Different from the way I always felt before."

"I guess I'm not the only one who does that."

"You said you were trying not to sound jealous."

"Trying."

Windy was quiet for a moment. "It was... magical. Almost like I could actually see him."

"Prometheus? The star of the play?"

"Yes." Windy had a dreamlike look in her eye. "It sounds stupid, but I almost wanted to climb onto the stage and set him free."

"Real stupid."

She just looked at him, feeling insulted. His words seemed harsh. "I know it wasn't real—"

"We're the last people who can say that," said PJ. "We don't know what's real and what's not real. We see shit that would make most people check themselves into a hospital."

"Prometheus is a myth—"

"So are the Haetae. Doesn't stop them from piggybacking on our brains and bodies and gobbling up five-alarm fires in the here and now."

Windy was suddenly defensive. "Well, it would be great if he was real. And maybe I would set him free. Why not? He gave people fire. And so we got samgyeopsal and ondol and lamps to place in the window to show people we love the way home—"

"I'd have gone insane."

"What?"

"Chained to a rock for thousands of years. An eagle eating my liver every single day. Insane. And pissed off." PJ took out a cigarette, tried and failed to light it. Finally gave up. "Not just at Zeus who put me there. But at humans too. Because I gave those bastards a light and look what happened. Look at the screwed-up world they made with it. And look what happened to me as a result of all my generosity, so-called." He shoved the unlit cigarette into his mouth. "Really, really, really pissed off."

The arson investigation team stared at their fire map and all the new data, including closeup satellite photos of the streets above the ghost station.

"Meteorological data shows no influx of air," said First Assistant Choi, "and no outgassing."

"It just went poof," said Second Assistant Cho.

"Not physically possible." Arson Investigator Kim, considered the confounding lack of meteorological anomalies on the streets above the underground blaze. "Fires don't go poof. Unless there was a blackhole at the origin point. And that's just not possible."

His cell phone buzzed and he answered it. "Kim here."

It was the police lieutenant, calling from his office as he stared at the photos of Windy Lee covered in pink fire retardant that were taken at the Cheongpyeong Forest fire. "We might have a match on your person of interest." A CCTV image taken just an hour previously showed Windy at the Namsan ticket booth with PJ Kwon.

Windy and PJ rode in the cable car with several other visitors, heading back down. They both stared quietly out the windows. PJ watched the station below as they approached, and saw Arson Investigator Kim, flanked by his two assistants and a pair of uniformed policemen.

He reacted to the sight of the welcoming party ahead, concluding correctly whom they were waiting for.

"Could you make that jump?" he asked Windy, indicating the slowly moving ground below them of trees and hard soil, perfectly willing to risk it. Windy saw the same folks at the station and considered PJ's proposal.

"No."

PJ seemed disappointed. "Looks like we're just gonna have to tell them the truth."

Less than an hour later, Windy and PJ were inside a police department interrogation room, seated at a plain table. Across from them was Arson Investigator Kim and a police interrogator.

"We turn into Haetae and put out fires," said PJ. "We're the first ones on the scene because Haetae have a nose for this kind of thing. So we're actually on your side. An unofficial department of the fire department. *First* first responders. If you think about it."

"It's the truth," said Windy.

Suddenly, ADMIN Yoon entered the room, guided by another police officer. "Good afternoon, Officers. Have charges been filed against my clients?"

Arson Investigator Kim turned to Windy and PJ, surprised, as they had not made any phone calls since they were detained. "Your attorney?"

"Is legal representation not every citizen's right?" said ADMIN. "To prevent abuses of authority? I take it they're free to go?"

Absent legal justification for holding them, the authorities in question just looked at him.

A few minutes after they had left, Arson Investigator Kim wheeled over to the window and stared outside, watching as Windy, PJ, and ADMIN got into the Beast and pulled away. He knew this was the same limo that had blasted by his van on the highway going to the Cheongpyeong Forest fire, the same vehicle that had pulled past him in the small-town hospital after that same fire. Yet another piece of the puzzle, but he had no idea what the overall image was supposed to be. And with each supposed clue, understanding seemed to get further away.

His phone buzzed. It was Coroner Gil. "We've got an ID from those Metro station fire casualties." Two badly charred bodies were laid out on the stainless-steel autopsy tables, in the coroner's lab, corresponding dental images displayed on a monitor nearby.

Arson Investigator Kim had mixed feeling about the identifications: one was a low-level habitual criminal who had been arrested several times previously for setting small businesses on fire for failure to pay a loan shark—that was not a surprise. The other was the famous CEO of Titanis Corporation, who was worth about a billion dollars—that was a shock.

In a moment, the big monitor in Kim's office displayed dozens of Navered photos of the dead arsonist:

holding press conferences, appearing at benefits, hosting visiting bigwigs. The logo of his Titanis Corporation accompanied most of the images.

Suddenly, Kim's gut ritual hypothesis seemed absurd.

Arson Investigator Kim took note of the same corporate logo as he wheeled himself inside the corporation's high-rise headquarters, flanked by his two assistants and closely followed by a half-dozen uniformed police officers. They all blew right past the security desk, into the elevators, and up to the main offices.

The receptionist tried to intercept. "Do you have an appointment?"

"We'd like to see CEO Kan's office please," announced Kim.

A vice president—VP Lim—moved to cut them off. "CEO Kan is not with us today," she said. "May I help you?"

"CEO Kan is no longer with us, period," answered Kim. He watched her reaction.

She seemed genuinely shocked. He showed her his identification badge, and explained that Kan had died in a fire. He did not mention that it was a fire the CEO had himself started. VP Lim showed them into a large corner office.

The dead CEO's suite had a full view of the Titanis Corporation's megatall skyscraper under construction halfway across the city. The space was also filled with dozens of classical images of Prometheus.

"What is Titanis currently working on?" asked Kim.

"High-tech solutions to the world's most pressing problems." It was a non-answer, but the Investigator didn't expect anything more. He just wanted to hear her tone of voice. To see if she might be hiding something.

Kim indicated a statue of Prometheus on the massive desk, which stood in for all the rest of them on the walls and in the alcoves. "And what is all this?"

The woman sighed wearily. "Everybody needs something to believe in."

Alone in his office later that same night, Arson Investigator Kim watched Firestarter Kan's YouTube channel, a series of public talks he gave and recorded that discussed the same hypothesis he had pitched to his corporate board. But at these various venues, he was much looser and among true-believing fans and fellow futurists.

"Did Prometheus steal fire from the gods and give it to humanity? For real? Sounds crazy. But let's rephrase: Did a being from an alternate universe bring advanced technology to Neolithic humans?" Supportive applause and laughter from his audience. "Doesn't sound quite as crazy, does it?"

Kim watched in wonder that any rational person let alone someone at the apparent top of a business career could carry on like this.

"And more to our point today: Could such a being do so again? Now? When we most need it? Reveal to us the next step in human technological evolution? How to let him know we are ready and willing? Maybe all we need to do is ask." The audience gave him a standing ovation.

The investigator hit pause, wanting a break from all this strangeness, or rather, madness.

Investigator Kim was awoken the next morning by a call from his assistants, who had also worked through the night, on the other side of town. "Sir, you should see this."

He took a taxi to a hangar owned by the Titanis Corporation. Inside, his staff showed him the holograph technology and associated cameras and recording devices. They turned it on and the holo-projection of Seoul appeared on the floor before them. Then they did a playback on one of the video machines, which showed the mudang performing her gut ritual dance above the 3D simulation of the city.

"I know her," said Kim, studying her face, which was mostly visible despite the blindfold she wore.

Back at the office, he gave her a call. "Manshin Mae. This is Investigator Kim, Seoul Metropolitan Fire and Disaster Management Headquarters."

"Hello, Investigator Kim. How can I help you?"

Her voice displayed no uneasiness or alarm at the call, which surprised the investigator for a moment. He still opted for a dishonest approach.

"We met briefly in Euljiro last week. At the gut you did for my sister. Golden Golbangi restaurant?"

"Yes, I remember."

"I could use your insights with a case I'm working on. I understand you have been consulted by law enforcement before?"

"Happy to do so. I have a two-tiered pricing system. One for a gut, another for consulting."

"Understood. We're interested in the latter, please. Would you mind coming into the office?"

"That's not a problem."

Three hours later, Arson Investigator Kim had a visitor.

"Hello, please let me introduce myself. I am Mathias Halko, professor of Folklore Studies, Aalto University, Finland currently on sabbatical in your fine city." It was not whom Investigator Kim had expected. He turned to First Assistant Choi who translated the newcomer's English into Korean for the benefit of the others. Then she continued to interpret the exchange between them.

"Pleased to meet you," responded Kim, hoping this surprise wouldn't last too long. "What is your business here?"

"I believe I may be of help to you," said the folklorist.

"How so?"

"I have studied the circumstances of the fires that have struck Seoul over the past several months. It is possible there is a not entirely natural explanation for how they were extinguished."

Kim was a little taken aback. He lied in response. "Those fires were put out by the fire department." There was no way an outsider—in Finland no less—could have learned that those blazes had all been quenched before the firefighters had finished their jobs.

"I have seen posts online that said otherwise."

"Such as?"

"Haetae."

The only reason Investigator Kim did not laugh out loud was the memory of his interrogation of the two young people he had escorted off the gondola coming down from Namsan Mountain. They had flippantly cited the same thing: Haetae. Was that a coincidence? Perhaps. But he was of the view that serendipity in law enforcement should never be dismissed outright. At least, it required a second look.

"Like the one on our logo?" asked Kim, indicating the fire department's emblem on the wall with the smiling Haetae caricature clearly depicted.

"Yes," answered the folklorist, who had seen it before.

"People can post anything online."

"True. But why *this*?"

Kim considered the Finnish scholar for a moment: his semi-formal suit, his confident but modest demeanor, the air of too much reading about him. And something else, some deep vulnerability that made Kim feel sympathetic toward Halko without knowing anything further about him. It was enough to justify more than a second look.

"Why are you in Seoul, Mister Halko? Did you come halfway around the world just to help me?"

"No."

"Please explain." At times, Arson Investigator Kim segued from interrogator to therapist, a move that on occasion got him closer to the information he was after, but on occasion just seemed to arise out of his natural empathy.

"I am seeking to prove a pet theory of mine."

"Go on."

"It is a bit technical."

"That's quite all right."

"The French philosopher Henry Corbin, in his studies of the medieval Islamic mystic Ibn 'Arabi, proposed a middle ground between the physical world that we perceive with our five senses and the pure world of ideas and thought. That realm he called the *Mundis Imaginalis*—Imaginal World—a place of 'immaterial matter' as it were, where dwell archetypal figures and image-ideas that have a kind of semi-independent existence distinct from the human imagination that helped call them into existence."

Kim glanced at First Assistant Choi who just shook her head no. She was not going to be translating that.

"What are the implications of your theory?" Kim asked instead.

"Haetae are real. And so are any number of so-called imaginary creatures and beings out of legend and myth."

Kim listened to the Korean translation of that declaration, then considered for a long moment. And for a tiny fraction of that moment, he thought there was something even more that Folklorist Halko was not telling him. Something deeper and more personal. But his empathy finally tapped out.

"Please let us exchange business cards," he said.

In the lobby of the building on the way to the street, Halko saw a woman entering. He recognized her, the famous Manshin Mae. She was even more striking in person than in her media coverage. He considered introducing himself, but before that impulse had formed enough to be acted upon, she had vanished into the elevator.

Investigator Kim showed Manshin Mae the same video he had seen several hours previously. She watched with a neutral expression the recording of her performance of the gut in the hangar, feet sweeping across the holographic display of Seoul.

"This is you?"

"Of course it is."

"You were employed by CEO Kan of Titanis Corporation."

"If you are asking that question, then you obviously know the answer."

"You know that he is dead."

The information barely registered on her face. "No. I haven't seen that on the news yet."

"It's not on the news yet."

"Why not?"

"We are still inquiring into the circumstances of his death. That being the case, we have not yet gone public with what is known."

The mudang didn't respond. In the same way Arson Investigator Kim had made a snap judgement of sympathy toward the wandering folklorist who had paid him a visit only minutes before, so he was instantly antipathetic toward the shamaness. She seemed made of ice and stone. Of course, that may well have been projection as the psychologists say. One calculating cynic onto another. He viewed himself as a rationalist in order to justify his own deep pessimism, but would not give her the same consideration.

"I could have you arrested as an accessory to arson."

"What are you talking about?"

"The ritual dances you performed for CEO Kan helped him pick out the locations of the fires that he started."

"Then I have been victimized as well."

"How so?"

Manshin Mae indicated the video of her gut, paused on a dramatic image of one of her dancing twirls. "He said he wanted me to find the most powerful locations in Seoul for a citywide gut that would invoke a spirit he called the Champion of Humanity. He said the information was proprietary and so he tied a blindfold over my eyes so I wouldn't see where the spirit told me to choose."

"You invoke any spirit your client requests?"

"That's my business model, correct."

"Even if that spirit, so-called, or your ritual performance itself, somehow informs major criminal activity?"

"I had no idea. He took advantage of my talent. That's obvious to you, as well, of course, or you would have already arrested me." She calmly stood away from the table. "I'll email you an invoice for my time."

The folklorist introduced himself the moment she stepped outside the doors of the fire department, where he had stood waiting for her, saying hello in Korean and giving his name.

"Use English, please," Manshin Mae responded, in perfect English.

He was taken aback, but heartened by the fact that they shared a language in which to communicate. "I am from Finland. A folklorist. I am here researching Korean mythological figures and shamanism. I saw an interview you gave on YouTube."

"Which one?" she said with a small smile.

"All of them."

"Ah. Okay." She considered the circumstances, and indicated the building behind them. "You saw me going inside?"

"Yes, as I was coming out. So I waited. Forgive me if that was uncomfortable behavior on my part," he said a bit awkwardly. "But a chance, if passing, encounter of such synchronicity seemed one that I should not ignore."

"I don't believe in synchronicity," said the shamaness. She was oddly charmed even though he wasn't trying to be charming. The same openness that had struck a sympathetic chord in Investigator Kim upon meeting the visitor from Finland had the same effect on her.

"But let's have coffee," she proposed, indicating the four appealing cafés that sat on each corner of the intersection in front of them.

"I have only been in Seoul a few days," he said. "All

the cafés in your city look equally wonderful to me."

She smiled. "All right. How about... that one?" She pointed to one of the four.

"Did a spirit tell you to make that choice?" he wondered aloud.

"The spirits are off the clock," she answered.

A few minutes later they sat across from each other in the café, espresso drinks and cakes in front of them.

"But surely there is shamanism in Finland?" Mudang Mae asked, after Halko revealed that he was hoping to hire one here in Korea.

"Indeed," he answered. "Among the Sami people, shamanism was an ancient belief system. There may well be a connection to practices in Korea. Perhaps even migration back and forth between the two lands as long ago as ten thousand years. But not as an active tradition today in Finland that outsiders can access. Not like you have here, where a shamaness such as yourself, employing methods handed down from the most ancient groupings of humanity, functions in seamless harmony with one of the most technological of the world's populations. It is quite astonishing, actually."

Manshin Mae considered him for a moment. She was born into a family of mudangs but had gone to college in the USA, at Arizona State University in Tempe, where she perfected her English, majored in psychology, and every couple of weeks found somebody to drive her to the other side of Phoenix and the lone Korean market in Arizona at the time. So she had the mudang's genetically inherited intuition, accentuated by her psychological training.

"You want to talk to your mother," she said suddenly.

He was taken aback to the point of shock. "As I said, I am here to do research."

She waited him out.

"But yes," he admitted, as if afraid to say the actual words, "I want to speak with my mother. She died when I was ten. How did you know that?"

"It's my business to know things like that. To guess things like that." Again, the shamaness considered him. Then decided on a course of complete honesty. "But I can't help you."

"I don't understand."

"There are *less* things in Heaven and Earth than are dreamt of in your philosophy," she amended the original Shakespeare. "With dance and music and the right frame of mind, I can generate in myself a willed, hypnogogic condition, and from there, semiautonomous complexes floating around in my brain can be given voice. Combined with what I know of you, and with my own intuition, that voice will anticipate the expectations you have…"

"And I will hear the words of my mother."

"Exactly."

"But it's not really my mother."

"I'm sorry."

Halko thought about that for a moment. "You are… not being honest with those who come to you."

"My work has a therapeutic effect. It helps people. So I don't consider what I do to be fraud. I'm a therapist who uses traditional methods of emotional healing and I've never had a single complaint. But there's nothing supernatural about what I do."

"You don't actually know."

"Know what?"

"That which you say is a 'semiautonomous complex' might actually be a spirit or a deity of some kind. Whether you acknowledge that or not would have no bearing on the result."

Manshin Mae had never entertained that idea. She suddenly smiled. "You got me there."

They enjoyed each other's presence in silence for a moment.

"You said your mother died when you were ten. Why do you want to speak with her now?"

"You do sound like a therapist."

"That's me. You don't have to answer."

He sighed. "I never told her that I loved her."

"A tough little boy."

"More like a little jerk."

"That's hard to imagine," she said.

"Everything she said and everything she did rubbed me the wrong way. I was always annoyed. And then she died. And..."

"And..."

"I saw the Swan of Tuonela, the Finnish Land of the Dead, take her away."

There was silence between them for a few moments. "A tough little boy with an active imagination," she finally said.

"It was as real as you are, sitting across from me. As real as that bus outside the window. As real as the sun in the sky."

"I can't say anything in support of that belief."

"I'm not asking for that. I don't need it. Nothing could make me doubt the truth of what I saw."

"I hope you don't mind that I can never believe you."

"You say it like we have some future together."

Manshin Mae smiled. "One more coffee at least."

Vice President Lim of the Titanis Corporation said goodnight to her assistant, who had stuck her head in the door to ask if she could stay. The group was not going out that night after work, the VP had told them to go home, that she needed to catch up on some business. But her assistant had been concerned about leaving her boss here alone after hours.

"It's alright," said the VP. "I'm never alone when I'm with my inspiration."

Her assistant nodded with admiration. "Good night."

"Good night."

After the young woman had left and closed the door, the VP went to the back of her office and pushed on a hidden panel, opening a large, walk-in closet that she had converted into a shrine.

To Athena, the ancient Greek goddess of wisdom and strategy in battle, which was to some, the highest form of wisdom.

When the VP had told Arson Investigator Kim that

"everybody needs to believe in something" she was deflecting attention away from herself. For just like Firestarter Kan, she too, *believed*.

She stepped into the shrine, surrounded by depictions of the deity, wearing her familiar bronze helm, holding the long spear in one hand, the aegis chest plate adorned with the head of a medusa ready for battle, an owl perched on her shoulder.

"Pallas Athena," chanted the Vice President of Titanis Corporation, "glorious goddess with the shining eyes, of thee I sing…"

"What?" asked Arson Investigator Kim, not believing what he had just heard.

"That person of interest we pulled off Namsan. Windy Lee. She was the baby who survived…" Second Assistant Cho's voice trailed off.

"Who survived the three-alarm fire that landed me in this wheelchair."

The assistant had not wanted to put it that way. But yes, that, apparently, was the case.

"I don't believe it," said Investigator Kim, even as he believed it.

"The name came up when I went into the physical files from back then," explained the assistant. "Stuff that hasn't been digitized yet."

"Only because we're too lazy to do it," said Kim, his mind elsewhere.

"Or too busy," chimed in First Assistant Choi, suddenly concerned by the distant expression on her superior's face.

"I'll see you tomorrow," he said unexpectedly, rolling himself toward the door.

"Do you want—" asked Second Assistant Cho, but his colleague shot him a look to silence the offer of a ride that was coming. If the inspector had wanted one, he would have asked for one. Instead, they both watched as Kim exited the office, the door closing behind him, wondering where the surprise invocation of the difficult past was taking him.

A two-hour drive directly south from Seoul put Arson Investigator Kim in the city of Gongju, former capital of the ancient Kingdom of Baekje, and more specifically on the side of a small hill where his wheelchair got stuck after he decided to go "off-roading" as he put it, as he often did. Firefighter Heo, retired, was up here picking wild perilla leaves for his table. Kim cursed at one of his wheels, loud enough for Heo to take notice.

"Been awhile," said the older man, looking over from his foraging and instantly recognizing his former colleague.

"Twenty-five years," agreed Kim.

"Wondered what took you so long."

A short time later, they were seated at a table outside the old man's small house at the bottom of the hill, drinking beer and snacking on pickled perilla and rice.

"What did you mean," asked Kim, "wondered what took me so long? 'Wondered' about what?"

"You know what."

"I really don't," lied Kim.

"Just ask me. Maybe I'll answer. It's probably been long enough."

Kim indicated the small rise behind the house. "What else do you pick up there?"

"Mushrooms. Acorns. Some cousin to ginseng."

"What did you see that night?"

"I had my eyes closed."

"What did you hear?" asked Kim.

"The fire, screaming, like it was scared shitless."

"That's a strange thing to say."

"You asked."

Kim stared at him, not believing but also having a hard time thinking he was lying. "People hear a lot of strange things when they're facing death."

"What did you hear?'

Kim didn't come here to remember that. "My heart beating so loudly that even the fire was drowned out."

"She laughed."

"What?"

"The baby. The little girl. I heard her laugh."

Retired Firefighter Heo had offered to join Kim in a visit to the city's main landmark, the tomb of King Muryeong, who had ruled Baekje until his death 1,500 years ago. Kim suspected this was not just politeness toward a surprise visitor out of the past, and so, despite wanting to get back in Seoul, he went along with it. The ancient tumulus was amazingly well-preserved because it had been discovered recently, in the seventies, untouched by grave robbers. Which meant all the grave goods that were buried with the king and his unnamed queen were found intact. Including one that had been left to guard the entry to the vault, the object Heo had wanted Kim to see.

There it was, in the museum adjacent to the tomb: a carved stone animal, thick body, scaled, lionlike face, and a single iron horn on its forehead.

"Haetae," said Kim.

"That's what I saw," said Heo.

"You said you had your eyes closed."

"I did. But I still saw it."

"What was it doing?" asked Kim, afraid to hear the answer.

"Eating the fire."

Investigator Kim wheeled himself around to take a closer look at the creature from the front. The requisite smile that the sculptor had left 1,500 years ago had not faded. As if it had been waiting for Kim all that time just to gloat.

Windy moved fast across the landscape, in the midst of an unseen pack of Haetae. The familiar sound of wolflike breathing and lionlike snuffling surrounded her. They were heading toward a mountain in the distance. But it appeared foreign to this landscape of green

hills and stone megaliths: more like a peak out of the ancient Caucasus mountain range. A sudden series of leaps—as if the pack was running and jumping at the same time—brought them closer to the mountain in a matter of seconds.

Prometheus stood on the side of the mountain, small fires all around him, free of his chains, arms outstretched in victory. Suddenly, he detonated.

And at a point five hundred meters in the air above Seoul, that dreamlike event became an explosion of nuclear force: blasting outward, the shock wave leveling the city with a firestorm.

Windy woke to find herself in the clubhouse sauna.

She was alone, vapor rising around her, greatly disturbed by what she had just daydreamed in her steamy reverie. Then she realized her phone had buzzed.

There was a message from Poet: a selfie of him five hundred meters above Seoul, on the top floor of the superstructure of the Tower of Olympus being built in Jongno. He was smiling and making a tiny heart with thumb and forefinger.

Windy threw on her clothes and exited the huge hanok and rushed along the street, looking for a place to catch a taxi at this late hour. She couldn't trust Driver Park to take her to Poet: too many questions would need to be answered. A taxi passed by and she flagged it down.

As they sped along the deserted streets, Windy, worried, pulled out the business card Arson Investigator Kim had given her when she was taken in for questioning.

Kim was asleep on the couch in his office, after having exhausted himself trying to work every angle of this case. His phone buzzed, and he checked his messages, finding a pic of the Tower of Olympus, just taken by Windy from the back of her taxi. The text said: "Hurry."

He hauled himself into his chair and down to his van, calling his team along the way. In a few minutes he was speeding northward and could see the Tower of Olympus ahead through his windshield: a reddish-yellow glow from the very top of the structure made it look like the flame of a gigantic candle. Had a fire just been started? He called it in and kept going.

When Windy's taxi reached the construction site of the immense building, she got out and rushed toward the gate of the wire fence blocking the entrance to the bottom floor of the open metal and concrete superstructure. The chain lock of the gate was already broken. She stepped through and moments later had located the work crew elevator and boarded it.

The elevator cabin was exposed on all sides: a working elevator meant for construction crews. As it rose—up, up, up—she had a dizzying view of the city before her.

That view was interpenetrated by flashes of the mythological world breaking into this one: the Neolithic Korean landscape of the Haetae, running with the pack as before, in the alpha position. Which gave way to the mountainous terrain of ancient Greek myth, and the Caucasus-like peak wreathed in clouds, finally revealing the rock to which Prometheus had been bound: only the broken chains remained.

The Titan had been freed.

DING. The elevator reached the top floor. Windy stepped out to see small fires burning all about the floor. She saw Poet standing near the edge of the unguarded precipice 150 stories above the street.

He was staring at the city below. And waiting for her. He turned and smiled. Poet took a few steps toward her—smoke rose up from every step he took, as it had for the smoking tiger, as if he somehow had fire inside his very body.

"You set him free," said Windy.

"Yes."

The small fires around them added to the sense of being simultaneously both in this world and in the next.

"PJ says Prometheus is so angry," said Windy, "that he's gone insane."

"He might be right."

"Then why…"

"That's why you are here," smiled Poet. "In case things go bad."

"I don't understand."

"The gift the Titan offers is too good to pass up."

"I didn't know you were so greedy."

"It's not for me. It's for everybody. Everybody in the world."

"Think too much about all this stuff and you start to think you're a god too. Everybody's savior. You're not. Give this up. Come home."

"I know you well enough by now. Love you enough. To know you won't disappoint me. You're the only one of us with the strength."

"To do *what*?" There was panic in Windy's voice.

"What needs to be done."

"You used me," she realized. "After all your pretty talk about love and trust and betrayal—you broke my trust and betrayed my love. You led me on and led me here—from the start."

"No. Not from the start. I did not know myself where

I was going. Until at last I understood."

"What? Understood what?"

"I want something more for us. A better world. Love isn't enough."

"It's enough for *me*."

Poet's eyes went glassy. "He's here."

Suddenly, the figure of Prometheus was superimposed upon that of Poet, and they become one and the same. In a kind of slow motion that to Windy's subjective eyes seemed to take ten thousand years, both his hands were raised in a kind of offering, holding a shimmering metallic globe covered in gears and wheels and tiny projections that seemed both ancient and of the unimaginable future to come. He tossed this mechanism toward Windy.

And at that moment, she was aware of a presence looming before her, its back turned to her. The creature turned and she saw its face, close to hers: single iron horn, big eyes, wide grin, as if encouraging her.

Then she too became a Haetae. And opened her massive maw.

Poet/Prometheus suddenly detonated—just as the Titan had done in Windy's dream—but she simultaneously absorbed the vast energy with a loud CHOMP: the void inside her, the black hole at the center of the Haetae, could eat anything, even the otherworldly equivalent of a nuclear blast.

A night security guard at Namsan Tower happened to be facing north from the lookout point at that very moment; from all the way across the city, it looked as though there was a gigantic candle, suddenly lit and instantly snuffed out.

Windy had been blown to the edge of the superstructure; all trace of fire or explosion was gone, and so were Poet and the Titan, both vanished. Dazed, she teetered on the edge, 150 floors above the street, then started to fall backward, sleeves singed, device in her hands, like a moth burned by a candle flame.

She vaguely heard the sound of wheels speeding across concrete. Arson Investigator Kim was propelling himself fast as he possibly could to reach her before she fell.

He had seen *something*. Blurred, hallucinogenic, but somehow terribly real. Something that went against all he believed—all he thought he knew—about how the world works.

Faster and faster, he tore the skin on his palms driving it so hard, closer and closer, he reached for her, cried out... as Windy went over the edge. The front wheels of his wheelchair stopped just short of the precipice.

He was devastated, but could only peer over the side and watch her fall.

And fall... and fall... and fall... far enough and long enough for the night skyline of Seoul to imprint itself on her brain, and for her to have time enough to think: this is the last thing I will see.

Suddenly, there was a rush of wind, and *something* caught her. She saw fragmentary glimpses of a long neck, multicolored pinions, great wings of black, white, red, green, and yellow, multiple tails, golden beak and talons, and heard a sound piercing the roar of the wind, like the cry of an enormous peacock.

And then she was on the ground.

An immense bird—the bonghwang of Korean mythology—the size of a Cessna, had carried her to safety. She watched as it settled onto the asphalt and then vanished, replaced by an athletic young woman who had been hosting the creature just as Windy and her colleagues host the Haetae.

"Did you think you were the only game in town?" laughed the woman, in reaction to Windy's stunned expression. She indicated the object she now held in her hands: the mechanism Poet had delivered from the Titan Prometheus. "I'll take this. Thanks."

A handsome young man riding a superbike roared into view, sliding to a stop. The young woman laughed again, jumped onto the back of the bike, and threw an arm around the rider's waist as they took off, disappearing from sight up the street.

Windy seemed to hear that laughter in her ears even after she couldn't see them anymore. Without thinking about it, she started to *run*, chasing after the woman who had both saved her and stolen the mechanism that Poet had apparently sacrificed himself to bring into this world.

And in a moment, she heard the familiar breathing and low growl of the pack she now was fully a part of, and she effortlessly became Haetae, bounding along the street, faster and faster. From her point of view the city surrounding her became superimposed over the mythological landscape of the ancient Korean peninsula, grassy hills and monumental stones.

At this late hour, there were still people out and about, as there always were in this liveliest of cities, small groups from the same business office on the third place or even fourth place of their extended restaurant crawl, couples heading home, and a trio of ajusshi seated on the porch of a convenience store drinking soju and talking into the night. Nobody saw anything except perhaps a distorted blur passing by: the most their conscious awareness, not attuned to the alternate universes, could perceive of the pursuit that flashed past them.

At one point, Windy saw a taxi turn quickly in front of her, putting itself between her and the woman on the motorcycle. But her speed did not slacken and she bounded forward, right through the taxicab, as if she or it was momentarily unsolid, or somehow the spaces between their constituent atomic particles had perfectly aligned to let one object pass unnoticeably through the other.

Another couple of moments and she was within bounding distance of the fleeing motorcycle. The woman with one hand around the rider's waist and the other holding the purloined mechanism suddenly seemed to feel the proximity, and turned just in time to see the Haetae leaping toward her, its maw wide open.

Shocked into action, she stepped off the back of the motorcycle into nothingness—and became again the huge bonghwang, simultaneously spreading its wings and clawing through the air.

Windy felt a surge of anger as she gave a final leap—and chomped down on a couple of tail feathers as the bonghwang escaped into flight. It shrieked in fury—and then was gone.

Windy landed on the asphalt, and found herself standing in the middle of the street, no sign or feeling any longer of the presence of the Haetae she had become.

Just then there a blast from a horn. She turned and saw the limo. Windy quickly reached for the handle of the rear door.

"Sit up front," said Driver Park. As if Windy had earned it. She got inside and saw that everybody was waiting for her: PJ, Hungry Gal, Admin, the Kid. Everyone except Poet. She closed the door behind her and Park wheeled them out of there.

Firetrucks and police cars had arrived at the base of the building. So had the two assistant arson investigators. Everybody stared upward, but there were no longer any flames. Investigator Kim himself finally wheeled out of the first floor, encountering the fire captain.

"Looked like an electrical short on the top floor," he lied. "Fires are out. Minimal damage." That was the truth. "Might want to double-check to be on the safe side."

Several of the firefighters headed into the building to do as he suggested. But there seemed no emergency here.

Kim maneuvered himself out to where he could examine the area where Windy would have hit the ground had she not been "miraculously" rescued. Of course, nothing was there.

And he wanted to keep what he had just seen— or imagined he had seen—to himself: a living Haetae consuming a ball of exploding fire, a mysterious device, a bonghwang diving in for a last moment rescue. He stared back up the side of the vast superstructure, which seemed to point all the way to the Heavens.

3. Ending

Motif Types

F721.2.2. Monster guards door of habitable hill.

A482. God of gambling (luck).

H942. Tasks assigned as payment of gambling loss.

D830. Magic object acquired by trickery.

F639.2. Mighty diver. Can stay extraordinary time under water.

D94. Transformation: man to ogre.

G317. Wrestling ogre.

D1330. Magic object works physical change

F531.6.15.1. Giants and gods in fight.

E323. Dead mother's friendly return.

A121.2. Sun as deity.

F531.6.12.1.1. Giant disappears in mist.

A192. Death or departure of the gods

"There were no tigers in ancient Greece, so the question of whether or when they smoked is a moot point. Mostly, those folks flattered whichever god they wanted some favor from: 'Sing Muse, of Hermes, son of Zeus and Maia, friendliest to man, guardian of dreams, god of luck and the best thief who ever was, help me steal this melon from this melon patch'—that sort of thing. As it happened, my encounter with the Titan blew a hole somewhere between the world of the Haetae and the world of the Olympians and our regular old world of corndogs and cat cafés. And the days of dealing with massive arsons and thugs on the subway seemed like a quaint and simple era."

Windy had been spending a lot of her spare time on the rooftop terrace—and like her fellow club members, she had nothing but spare time—staring at the lights of the city and letting the twinkling near and far set her thoughts adrift, slipping into a reverie where one imagines and is imagined at the same time, and so the forces acting from her and acting upon her were balanced into a kind of bridge. It was that bridge that allowed her more and more easily and naturally to access the realm of the Haetae. And running with them, *as* one of them, had become her greatest pleasure and escape.

It was during one of these runs that she became aware of a figure moving quickly before the pack, out ahead of them, seeming to almost dance and fly and run at the same time. Windy realized that she and her fellow Haetae had been somehow entranced into following, as if they were being *led*. Windy took a closer look and the figure came more clearly into view: a young Korean man with a handsome and mischievous face who seemed delighted to have taken control of the direction of the pack.

Windy was instantly annoyedly. She immediately turned to side and the rest of the Haetae followed her lead, pulling them away from their would-be shepherd. It was his turn to be annoyed. He did a backwards somersault, landing right on Windy's shoulders, and she could feel him grip the iron horn in the middle of her forehead and try to forcibly steer her in the other direction.

She bucked like a bronco and he held on like a rodeo rider until she charged straight for a dolmen. The unwelcome "cowboy" barely had time to leap off in a panic before she smashed right into the stack of massive stones, scattering them like pebbles.

And knocking herself out of the land of the Haetae and back to her rooftop—where the erstwhile rider had also landed, rolling hard and smashing against the side of the terrace.

He sat up straight and she got a better look at him: still handsome in the harsh light of the real world, midtwenties, wearing a track suit and Nike "Aunt Pearl" sneakers with noticeable wings worked into the Velcro straps.

"On Day One of my immortal life," he exclaimed, delighted, "I stole the sacred cattle owned by my brother. Establishing for all time my bona fides as consummate cowherd and thief without equal in all the cosmos. And yet *you*, with your herd of... of... what exactly *were* those things?"

"Haetae."

"Haetae. Have outwitted even me. How... how *marvelous*." He had suddenly seen and reacted with wonder to the sight of the city lights below. "Not Babylon nor Persepolis in their glory could have held a candle to this. Is this Heaven on Earth?"

"It's Seoul."

The young man seemed baffled.

"Republic of Korea."

He still had no clue.

"What are you?" asked Windy.

"Hermes, son of Zeus and Maia the nymph, brother to Apollo, slayer of Argos, messenger of the gods of Olympus. Hermes... *Lee*," he decided, choosing a surname appropriate to the environment.

"*Mercury?*"

"Bite your tongue. Cheap Roman knockoff."

"What are you doing here?" asked Windy, still annoyed with his interference.

"That's it? No awe?"

"I just threw you halfway across the universe."

"True. And don't think I don't respect that," answered Hermes. "I'm here to take back some gizmo that Hephaestus had lying around his workshop."

"*Vulcan?*"

"What did I just tell you about Italian imitations?"

"Sorry."

"You should be: it was you that the Titan tossed it to, before his unfortunate... detonation."

"I don't have that thing anymore. A bonghwang took it from me."

"A what?"

"A big bird. Local."

"What does it look like?"

"Hang on..." Windy Navered the creature on her phone, coming up with an image of the seal of the president of the Republic of Korea featuring a pair of gold-colored bonghwang facing each other.

"Oh, look at that." He was marveling at a huge advertising display projected across the faces of three office buildings in the distance.

"Do you want to see this or not?" she said, holding up the screen displaying the mythical bird.

"I want to explore."

He leapt off the roof and vanished into the lights in the distance.

The folklorist from Finland, Matthias Halko, had found a one-room officetel in Gwanghwamun, in order to be close to the big statues of the two Haetae that guarded the gate to the palace grounds with its museum and daily traffic of visitors. He went to greet the pair every morning after waking up, then went for a walk through the palace itself, impressed every time by how built to human scale it was. Not intended to overawe like the ruling residences of the ancient world, of China or Egypt, whose rulers might style themselves as Sons of Heaven or even deities, but to provide a Confucian example to those they ruled. He wished he *lived* here.

One day, his walking took him into the evening, south and then east of the monumental sculpture of King Sejong that Great that was the central focus of the neighborhood.

He found himself in a narrow alleyway running parallel to a major and busy avenue. With barely enough room for two people to walk side by side, the alley was, surprisingly, lined with tiny restaurants.

This pathway was not on any of the online maps that he always consulted, and so neither, of course, were any of the eating establishments. It started to rain and he looked among the storefronts for a convenience market that might have sold umbrellas. Not immediately finding one, he gave up the search. The ambient temperature was neither cold nor hot and the raindrops felt good, even after his head was soaked. He just kept walking in the rain, looking inside every restaurant he passed, where the occupants seemed inevitable: wife and husband owner, one or two friends or regular customers talking and eating with them. It was like a kind of parallel village that ran alongside the busy metropolitan avenue, and struck him as being one of the things that had attracted him so profoundly to Seoul: the combination of comfortable, familiar, local dynamics in the midst of the most modern and technological of cities.

That quality is what had attracted him to folklore itself: the local. Some people felt the need to be a part of something much greater than themselves. Halko wanted more than anything to be part of something *small*.

His native Finland had no lack of grand narratives.

The epic poem Kalevala, compiled in the nineteenth century from older tales of folklore and myth, was one of the world's grandest: so culturally compelling as an origin tale of the Finnish people that it actually informed the movement that led to Finnish independence from Russia.

But the tales that frequently stuck in Halko's imagination were barely tales at all, but moments and images: snapshots, as it were, singular observations of the odd and the uncanny that had been passed down for generations, that did not even demonstrate so much as a plot let alone something that might be called a story.

Not unlike, if he would have expanded his parameters to include the deeply personal, the vision he had had of the black swan of Tuonela, the Land of the Dead, as it carried off his dying mother—the experience that had set him on his present course. Of course, he would not have admitted that. Because if he had, that might mean that his life's work, his attempt to prove the reality of mythical figures by way of the Imaginal world, was not based on the quality and validity of the ideas, but was driven instead by the little boy inside him who still mourned and missed his mother, who needed desperately to know she still existed somewhere, still thought about him, still loved him.

A large, solidly built, handsome Korean man drank

several bottles of Hite and shots of whiskey one after the other, setting them back on the bar with surprising politeness given his burly aspect and the circumstances. Despite appearing to be in his fifties and therefore far too old for this Gangnam hip-hop club, his natural charisma had made him instantly and even shockingly popular at the vast, packed venue on this particular night. He had already had half a dozen erotic encounters at various locations throughout the space, and gave no indication of quitting while he was ahead.

A young woman, model appearance, playfully counted all the empties in front of him and enticed him to follow her outside to the back of the building. And there, a bouncer she knew, whose girlfriend the large man had momentarily but successfully seduced an hour previously, smashed him on the side of the head with the blunt end of a small fire axe, splitting his skull wide open.

The large man was completely caught by surprise and stumbled off into the night, still on his feet despite a gaping wound in his head that should have put him in the hospital if not the crematorium.

A couple of young toughs watched amazed as he staggered off, and considered going after him to check if he was wearing a watch or still had his wallet.

Three alleys away, the large man finally dropped, landing hard on his side and rolling on the ground before coming to a rest.

At that moment, the open crevasse in his skull showed movement from inside. *And an infant girl crawled out of his head.*

She clambered over his supine body and pulled herself wriggling across the alley toward a dumpster.

"Did you see that?"

"I'm gonna be sick."

The two toughs from the back of the nightclub had finally gotten up the nerve to follow after the big man.

"Can't be real."

"Let's go look."

"No chance."

"Come on."

They paused at the fallen giant's body—incredibly, he was still conscious and groaning—took his wallet and cash and then, with trepidation and morbid curiosity, headed toward the dumpster where the infant had apparently hidden herself.

When they got there, a severely beautiful, permanently unsmiling Korean woman in her midthirties stood before them, wearing a narrow leather skirt and a Versace blouse with the Medusa logo emblazoned across the front.

She raised her hand and suddenly an extremely long spear was in her palm. She gripped it tightly and swept it to the side, striking both the men at once and sending them flying into the nearest wall. They did not get up or even stir.

"Father." The woman turned toward the fallen man, but he was no longer there. And she had no way to track him.

She considered for a moment, then suddenly vanished into thin air.

The large man with the hole in his head walked into a mom-and-pop, all-night pharmacy, so small that he filled the entire waiting area when he stepped through the door.

"What do you have for a headache?" he asked.

"Advil and Tylenol," answered the old woman behind the counter.

"All right."

She finally looked up at him, saw the massive head wound and handed a small rectangular box of each analgesic across the counter without batting an eye. The large man shoved both boxes into his mouth, not bothering to open them, and swallowed them down as the old woman watched.

"I don't have money," said the man.

The old woman took out a ledger, handing him a pen and indicating where to write. "You can open a tab," she said. "Sign it and pay the next time you are in."

The man wrote his name: *Zeus Lee*.

"Thank you," he said. "You are very kind."

The old woman shook off his compliment with a grumble. The man considered her for a moment. "Your grandson will take over your business," he finally announced, "and it will thrive."

The old woman laughed. "That lazy boy wants nothing to do with this place."

"He will come around. But not until you are dead."

His bluntness was shocking but the old woman didn't seem to care. "Just my luck."

"Luck has nothing to do with it," said the large man. "The destiny of a mortal is woven by the Three Sisters of Fate. Clotho spins the thread, Lachesis takes its measure, Atropos cuts it off. There is no way to change this."

"What do *you* know?"

"What *don't* I know?" came the weary response, tinged with melancholy, as Zeus Lee exited the shop and returned to the night, ready, despite the crease in his skull, to continue the party.

A tiger swam deep under the water, comfortably, as if it were a dolphin or a shark that belonged there.

"Once, when tigers dove for abalone, the Dragon King in his underwater palace, who had feasted night and day for centuries, finally got sick from overindulgence. His underwater doctors consulted their starfish oracles and were told that the only cure was the liver of a rabbit but as rabbits did not live underwater, one of the hired hands would have to go find a suitable candidate topside. The assignment went to Turtle as the crappy jobs always did, and so he climbed out of the water and asked around as he had never seen a bunny before, and eventually somebody pointed out Rabbit, napping in the sun after a night out on the town, surrounded by empty bottles of hangover cures. Turtle waited patiently until Rabbit woke up and then introduced himself and said that the Dragon King's underwater palace had free food and drink as much as you could want and invited Rabbit to come on down. Turtle didn't feel bad about saying any of that because it was all true—he just left out the part about the liver. Headache notwithstanding, Rabbit wasn't going to say no to such an invitation. So down they went, through the waves and past the seaweed and behind the coral to the underwater palace, where the Dragon King and his staffers all cheered the rabbit and broke out the beer and anju. Rabbit had been going at it

for hours until he finally noticed that the Dragon King was just sort of pushing his food around and pretending to drink. Rabbit asked if anything was wrong, and Dragon King admitted he was terribly ill and only a rabbit's liver could fix things and, well, did he really have to spell it out? Rabbit said No problem at all! That caught everybody off guard. But unfortunately, he told them, he had consumed so many highballs yesterday that he had to hang his liver out to dry. If Dragon King could wait here a bit, Rabbit would go and get it. Knowing zero about rabbits or life above the sea or even pretty much anything beyond his own underwater palace, Dragon King commanded Turtle to go along and make sure Rabbit kept his word. So off they went, back up to the surface. Once they got to Rabbit's place, Turtle asked where the liver was and Rabbit laughed, My liver is exactly where it's always been. Turtle tried to grab him but it was impossible. Rabbit laughed again and said: your Dragon King didn't even know that on dry land rabbits are a hundred times faster than a turtle—you'll never catch me. Turtle could see it was true. He also realized that if he returned to the underwater palace as the bearer of bad news, all the blame for this fiasco might fall on him. So he didn't. And the Dragon King is still down there, waiting for him.

And so, when Aphrodite Lee emerged from the sea foam breaking picturesquely against the reef on one of the tiny islands off Jeju, like Botticelli's Venus on the half shell, the tourist who was passing by on a rented bicycle hoping to see 'the last generation of Korea's living mermaids' took one look and thought, That's the most beautiful woman I have ever seen, they must be doing a photo shoot around here. Haenyeo Pang thought, If that's what a turtle from the Dragon King's Palace looks like nowadays, then I'd better watch my liver. But Haenyeo Nam, her younger cousin by one month, didn't just think, but said out loud, 'The daughter I lost twenty years ago has come back to me.' And it was her still-broken heart that decided what happened next."

Needless to say the diving was over for the day. The two cousins took the ferryboat ride to the main island with their catch: a small octopus, some sea urchins, a bunch of sea snails, handfuls of seaweed and the Greek goddess who looked like a Korean supermodel.

Haenyeo Nam spoke to her as if nothing was amiss, as if indeed, the ten-year-old child she had lost to the waves had just reappeared out of the blue sea, and was eager to be caught up on the local news.

"Your father died five years after you left," said the woman. "Of course I didn't remarry. There are not a lot of fish in this sea." She said it jokingly, in reference to the ferryboat operator and one of his friends, at sixty, both her peers. They laughed with good humor. She indicated her cousin. "Your auntie and me just kept diving. But the waters are always changing. Some years there's a lot of this, some years a lot of that. Lately though, there's been a lot of *nothing*."

But her cousin sat with a stony expression and would not even look at the newcomer.

"I see," said Aphrodite.

"And what have you been doing all this time?" asked the woman who had claimed her as her daughter.

"Oh, this and that," the newcomer said brightly, imitating what she had just heard.

"We don't have any extra room," said her cousin suddenly.

"She'll sleep with me," insisted the other woman, who moved off momentarily to check on their wetsuits that they had hung over the boat's railing to dry in the sun.

"If you hurt my cousin," said Haenyeo Pang, "I'll drown you like a rat."

"I am born of the waves and deathless, so that would not be possible," said Aphrodite, without rancor or attitude, as a pleasant statement of fact. "But you are welcome to try." Her smile was so pretty that the other woman had to turn away.

The ferryboat operator couldn't help but stare. But

he was not staring at the Goddess of Beauty: he only had eyes for Haenyeo Pang, a dynamic that Aphrodite perceived instantly, as the patroness of love missed nothing in that regard, no matter how small, no matter how repressed, no matter how unrequited.

At their apartment in Hongdae, the young woman who had channeled the bonghwang onto the streets of Seoul was examining the mysterious mechanism she had grabbed from Windy, as her boyfriend, the motorcycle rider, looked on.

"What does it do?" he asked.

"No idea." She tried moving the various geared wheels along the surface of the volleyball-sized metallic sphere, but could not seem to activate it or indeed, generate any kind of response. Frustrated, she tried bouncing it on the floor—it just hit the tiles and seemed to sit there.

"My second cousin teaches chemistry at Yonsei," said her boyfriend.

"So what?"

"So maybe he can put it into an X-ray machine or pour some acid on it or something."

"What's that gonna do?"

"Might tell us what's inside or what it's made of."

That didn't seem like too bad of a suggestion, but she didn't want to actually say so.

The second meeting between Folklorist Halko and Manshin Mae was their first real date. She had wanted a cocktail bar whose head bartender had been trained in some allegedly special shaker technique by a famous mixologist in Tokyo, but he was just hoping for some makgeolli. Both was her answer. And a third place after the first two. He said yes to that. And just kept saying yes for some reason he didn't quite understand, to everything. When she spent the night the first time she never left. He said yes to that, or rather, didn't say no. When on a double date with her best friend—another mudang and her fiancé—the woman had asked him about wedding plans: Would he and Manshin Mae be married by next spring? He said that seemed about right, even though he and the mudang had never even mentioned marriage. It was just yes, yes, and again, yes.

He was quietly happy with his new life in Seoul, but she wouldn't let him slack off his goal—uncovering the reality of the Haetae—even if she, herself, didn't believe it for a minute.

"There has to be a mudang involved," she said, seemingly out of the blue.

"What are you talking about?" he asked.

"If the Haetae are really doing things in the real world, really and truly putting out actual fires, then somebody had to bring them here. They can't just show up on their own. There has to be a gut, or at the very least, a powerful mudang who doesn't even need a gut to function."

"How can you say that when you believe that the spirits you invoke yourself are nothing but psychological complexes?"

"I'm open to the idea that a psychological complex could be projected onto the world outside by way of a psychokinetic effect."

"The Haetae are the visual embodiment of somebody's psychokinesis?"

"Just an idea."

He considered for a moment. "How would I find them?"

"The mudang who are calling down the Haetae?"

"Yes."

"Give a lecture."

So that's what he did. Scheduled a talk at Yonsei University called "Haetae are real: mythological figures and the *Mundus Imaginalis*" and advertised it all over the internet, even went around town with his fiancé—for he and Manshin Mae were now engaged—and put up flyers. It was fun. Even if he didn't expect anything would come of it.

But on the day of the lecture, Windy Lee, ADMIN Yoon and Driver Park were in the audience, wondering if Finnish Folklorist Matthias Halko knew too much, and if so, what to do about it.

Bonghwang Rider and her boyfriend were blasting along the streets toward Yonsei University, the mysterious piece of technology stowed in a backpack slung across her shoulder.

As they sped toward the parking lot, she was shocked to see an athletic woman suddenly appear directly in front of them, wearing a Versace blouse with the unmistakable Medusa logo, holding a three-meter-long spear that was pointed right at them.

Her boyfriend jerked the bike hard to the left to avoid a collision. The tip of the spear stabbed through the spokes of the front wheel, sending the motorcycle flipping back over front. The young man went flying, and when he hit the ground it was with so much force that his helmet cracked in two—he rolled to his feet and ran away.

Still falling, the young woman shouted in anger at the retreat of her companion, but before she could hit the asphalt, she suddenly became the bonghwang, and her annoyance became a shriek of avian rage.

The creature turned in midair on the woman who had attacked them, grabbed hold of the long spear in its beak, and shook its long neck like a whip, tossing the warrior woman back and forth. It finally snapped its head with great force and opened its beak, sending the woman crashing along the campus grounds at high speed, where she still managed to keep hold of her great spear, but with a look of absolute surprise on her face.

No students or visitors or any potential witnesses perceived anything of this furious battle beyond a motorcycle that had apparently lost control and crashed. Unless they were psychically sensitive, in which case, for a few seconds, they saw everything but simply did not believe their eyes, because surely the nonstop study and lack of sleep was now resulting in hallucinations.

Folklorist Halko repeated his usual themes at the lecture: the Imaginal world and the real presences of mythological figures who were fashioned by human imagination and yet had themselves guided that same imagination by way of preexisting potential forms.

Manshin Mae was in the audience as were a scattering of students and a few professors politely showing their support for a visiting scholar, despite no interest in the topic.

Halko took questions afterward, and one student asked about the sources of his inspiration. "Vladimir Propp," cited Halko, "in his *Morphology of the Folktale*, wrote that 'in much the same way that we can use astronomical laws and the gravitational fields of known bodies to predict the existence of stars that we cannot see, it is also possible to assume the existence of tales we have not yet collected.' I found that notion compelling, even intoxicating. It suggested to me the possibility of uncovering or recreating the very first story that humans told to each other."

He let the idea sink in for a moment, as he himself also considered the words anew in light of his unexpected connection with Mae.

"Perhaps," he speculated, "the various stories of our own lives can point to an as-of-yet unlived tale, something waiting for us, a story we are circling around, something essential that we have not yet found."

He and the mudang smiled at each other.

"May you all find the stories that are waiting for you," he concluded with a sense of unexpected happiness.

Again, he considered his new fiancé and wondered if maybe his pursuit of mythical monsters was not the essential thing, that maybe he had found what he had truly been searching for without having known it, that he had journeyed to Seoul for one thing, but had discovered the real thing instead.

Then a multicolored bird the size of a city bus flew by the window, chased by a woman with a very long spear in her hands.

The bonghwang flipped completely around—performing an inside loop in stunt plane terminology—caught the attacking woman off guard and buried a talon into her momentarily exposed thigh. The woman roared in pain and fury.

"Good God, are you seeing this?" said Halko who had rushed outside, followed by his puzzled fiancé.

"No," answered Manshin Mae.

"How can you not? It's right there!" He pointed at the combatants, but the mudang saw nothing but grass, sidewalk, and air.

"*What* is right there?"

"A huge bird! Black, white, red, yellow, and green! With a neck like a python! Fighting a woman wearing Versace and wielding a spear!"

The shamaness could not stifle a sigh.

"You don't believe me?" he continued.

"I believe you *think* you are seeing something. And I can acknowledge and respect that."

Suddenly, the warrior woman planted herself on the ground and flung her great spear with such speed that the bonghwang could only twist its huge body in response, protecting its vulnerable underbelly, but not getting entirely out of the way: the spear penetrated an exposed wing and went right out the other side.

The bird's flight suddenly stalled, and it fluttered towards the ground—a second before it landed, the creature transformed back into the athletic young woman who had hosted it.

"Bitch!" she screamed, holding her now-wounded arm.

At that instant, Windy and ADMIN lifted her off the grass and rushed her into the Beast, which Driver Park had already thrown into gear.

Folklorist Halko watched them from a few meters away. He hesitated, but only for a moment. Then he grabbed hold of Manshin Mae's hand and pulled her along with him—both completely uninvited—into the limo along with the rest.

As the limo roared off Yonsei campus onto the surface streets, Bonghwang Rider screamed at her rescuers. "Let me out!"

But her arm was bleeding horribly. ADMIN had already accessed an onboard first-aid kit and was binding her wound. She was angry but didn't resist the treatment.

"What are you doing?" said Windy to the folklorist and the mudang.

"This is proof!" exclaimed the Finn. "I was right!" He turned to his fiancé. "I'm right! It's real! It's real!"

"What's real?" said Windy.

"You! All of you!"

"No shit," exclaimed Bonghwang Rider.

"You didn't see what you thought you saw," said the mudang.

"That's where you're wrong!" said Halko in his excitement.

His fiancé took offense. "So I don't matter?"

"Of course your opinion matters. But it's just one data point—"

"That was all just psychokinesis," insisted Mae, indicating bonghwang. "She was projecting the big bird. Somebody *else* was projecting the warrior with the spear."

"I must say," added ADMIN suddenly, "there is no way to prove you are wrong."

"Thank you," said the mudang.

"Of course, she's wrong!" Halko insisted, unwilling to

back off now that his life's work had finally been justified. "You know it too!"

"Let me out of the car," said Manshin Mae.

"Great idea," said Windy. "A lover's spat? *Now*?" She turned and shouted at Driver Park. "Stop the car." Back to the young woman with the wounded arm: "Get out." To the two lovers: "You too. Everybody out."

"I remember you!" said the bonghwang medium. "You bit half my tail feathers off!"

"You stole my thing!" Windy suddenly was aware of the backpack that was still draped around bonghwang's neck. "Is this it? Is this what you took from me?"

They started fighting over it. "How did you even know about us?" yelled Windy in midstruggle.

"You have a damn clubhouse," was the reply. "How hard can it be?"

At that moment, a spear pierced the roof and stabbed right between them. They all screamed.

Outside, the warrior woman was standing on the top of the speeding limo, jabbing repeatedly with her weapon through the roof, hoping to strike flesh or bone.

Inside the limo everybody instinctively grabbed for the shaft of the spear, trying to take hold and stop the stabbing. But it was no use. The woman on the rooftop was too strong. Up and down went the weapon, the metal of the rooftop shrieking with each stab, the screaming inside getting louder and more desperate.

"I thought this car was bulletproof!" shouted Windy.

"It is!" replied Driver Park.

"How is this happening?" continued Windy.

"It's the goddess Athena!" exclaimed the folklorist.

They all looked at him incredulously, despite the dire situation that took no pause.

"What?" shouted Windy.

"Of course," said ADMIN. "The *aegis*." He was referring to the Versace logo of the medusa: the same head that had adorned the indomitable breastplate of the ancient Greek goddess.

Another stab. This time, the tip of the spear went through ADMIN's pants, grazing his skin. "We have to get out of here."

But Windy shouted, "Unlock the door!" And Driver Park instantly complied. Windy kicked the door open with her foot—and rolled out of the speeding vehicle.

"I had never actually done anything like that before: a really stupid move that would hurt a lot at the very least. Basically, a challenge to the Haetae: put up or shut up. Come to me now or throw me to the wolves, as it were. You decide."

Before she hit the asphalt, she had become Haetae.

The massive creature rolled across the street, came up on its feet, and in one bound, landed with open jaws on top of the limo. Before the woman with the aegis on her designer t-shirt could even register its presence, the Haetae had snapped her spear—fashioned by the blacksmith of the gods, Hephaestus himself, forged of the hitherto unbreakable atoms of adamantine—in two.

The goddess Athena—for that indeed was what and who it was—desperately, and practically in shock, managed to keep hold of both halves of the shattered weapon as she leapt clear, trying to escape.

The last thing she saw, before the limo sped away, and before her monstrous assailant vanished, was its grin, which struck her as inexplicably friendly, despite their fierce encounter.

At the little home on Jeju Island, Aphrodite joined in the work, assisting the two cousins as they deshelled the catch for sale and decided to cook the octopus for themselves. The Olympian who had infamously kicked off the Trojan War—by promising an indecisive young shepherd the most beautiful woman in the world in marriage if he proclaimed Aphrodite the most beautiful goddess in Heaven—seemed utterly content with what, in comparison to those heroic, Homeric machinations, was the simplest of activities.

Haenyeo Nam talked nonstop, mostly gossip, who had married whom, who had been born, who had died, who had grown up and given up diving and moved to the mainland. She thought that if she stopped talking this gift would go away as suddenly as it came, and she would be alone again with only her cousin and her inconsolable grief.

For her part, Aphrodite felt the woman's words, trivial and meaningless as they might seem to an outsider, wash over her like incense and balm, and the lover of smiles herself could not stop smiling.

Haenyeo Pang watched from across the room, where she cut and fried the octopus. She thought she might be even more tired than she felt, because for a moment, it seemed as if the sea snails that the newcomer were deshelling were actually climbing willfully if not joyfully out of their exoskeletal homes to make it easier for her.

Titanis Corporation vice president Lim was in the middle of a busy day at the office, eyes already red from shifting from computer screen to hard copy and back again.

Her assistant buzzed in. "Vice President Lim?" Her voice was hesitant.

"I said no interruptions," was the VP's curt answer.

"You have a visitor."

"No I don't," insisted the VP.

"I don't know what to do," quavered the assistant's voice.

Puzzled, Lim looked up—in time to see the door fly open and a woman wearing a narrow leather skirt and designer t-shirt move inside like she owned the office, the building, the neighborhood, even the entire *polis*. She tossed two halves of a broken spear onto the couch and sat down.

"Who…?" stammered the VP.

"How can you not know me? You have sung my praises often enough."

Lim could not believe it, even as she said it. "Pallas Athena."

The deity considered her for a moment, then indicated the door. "I discomforted your fellow citizens. Forgive me. I should have… *made an appointment*." She said the words as if she had learned the concept very recently and was just now trying the idea out. "But now that I am here, I require some information."

"Anything, yes, what is you want to know?"

"What is the name of the indomitable creature who came at me? And," she asked incredulously, "broke my spear?"

"What did it look like?"

Athena went to the window and stared outside. She indicated the traffic going by. VP Lim came over for a look. The first thing she saw was a taxi with its haechi logo on the door.

"A Haetae?" She laughed.

"Is my misfortune in battle amusing to you?"

"Athena can't be beaten in a one-on-one fight."

"You are correct. But I faced *two* opponents. Not one. There was also a phoenix or possibly a roc out of Persia. And I was not defeated. But I did choose to execute a timely retreat."

"A giant bird? Like this?" She grabbed a newspaper off the desk and showed her visitor an article with a photo of the president doing a press conference behind a podium adorned with two facing bonghwangs.

"Yes, that was it. A giant bird and a lion-dog."

"Why did they attack you?"

"I attacked *them.*"

"Ah." VP Lim was starting to wonder about the reality not just of the woman in her office, but her own sanity. Was she really having this conversation?

"I was trying to retrieve the mechanism. That Prometheus stole from the workshop of Hephaestus."

The corporate executive was suddenly excited. "Yes?"

"Yes, stole. And it ended up in the hands of citizens of this city for whom it was not intended."

"For whom *was* it intended?" asked Lim, barely daring to hope for the answer she so wanted to hear.

"You, of course."

"Ah."

"Did you not ask for it? You and your vanquished partner?"

"Yes, we did." VP Lim wondered about Athena's motivation. "But the mechanism belongs to the gods."

Athena brushed it off. "I have always been a friend to those who love invention."

"The mechanism…?"

"… is one of the greatest of *all* inventions."

The VP laughed with joy. "I feel so… lucky to be a part of this—"

"Do not invoke luck," warned Athena. "Hermes is

the god of luck, and theft and mischief and a lot of other things. He is the last Olympian we want sticking his caduceus in our business right now."

"*Our* business?" repeated the Korean woman.

"Yes. 'Our.' In the same way I favored the clever Odysseus in his travels and travails, so I am on your side."

"Because I repeated some poems about you? From three thousand years ago?"

"Because I like your style. Do not question too much the affections of a god."

The mortal woman quashed her lingering doubts as directed. And then got to the business at hand. "Where is it?"

"It was in the hands, or the talons rather," admitted Athena, "of the great bird. After I abandoned the field."

"Well, then," said VP Lim, her confidence rising to meet these momentously unusual circumstances, "we will have to find it." She turned to the nearest computer and started opening the personal files of her dead boss.

In the basement of Club H, on the bare floor and around the ancient stone circle—the safest and most easily defended location in the house—everybody looked at the object that had been taken from the backpack: the mechanism stolen from the workshop of the immortals.

"So what is it?" asked Windy.

"I don't even know," answered Bonghwang Rider. "We did everything to turn it on. Maybe it needs new batteries."

"Who is we?" asked ADMIN.

"My boyfriend. My *ex*-boyfriend. He took off the second that chick showed up with the spear."

"It is the *Sampo*," said the folklorist with awe. "The Sampo of Ilmarinen."

The others all turned to him, no idea what he was talking about. Manshin Mae translated everything he said into Korean for their benefit.

"Do continue," encouraged ADMIN.

"In Finnish mythology, it is a singular invention, the theft of which drives the narrative of the *Kalevala*, our national origin tale."

"What does it do?" asked PJ.

"Three things it can make without ceasing," answered Halko. "Flour for baking—"

"Bingo," said Hungry Gal in English.

"Salt," continued the folklorist, "and gold."

"That's plenty," said the Kid.

"But this is Greek," said Windy, indicating the device, "right?"

"If indeed it was Prometheus who stole it," agreed ADMIN.

"The flour, the salt, even the gold are considered metaphoric," explained the folklorist. "It simply means that the device in question can produce infinite bounty for humankind. The Sampo represents in mythic terms any invention that can promise unlimited benefit for its user."

"It's still mine," said the bonghwang lady. "I earned it fair and square."

"You took it from me," said Windy.

"In return for saving your life."

"In the classical Greek tradition," continued Halko, "Prometheus did not bring fire to any single individual. He gave it to humanity as a whole." The folklorist indicated the mysterious mechanism before them. "Sampo or fire—again, it is figurative speech. It represents some kind of technological knowledge that allows human beings to advance, even to rival the gods themselves."

"Sounds like it belong to all of us," said PJ.

"If you can keep it," chimed a musical voice. They all

turned at the newcomer: an extremely handsome Korean man in his thirties, well dressed. He had not come down the ladder from above but had materialized into their midst. He held a small branch in one hand.

"Who in the world are you?" asked Hungry Gal, as if enough was enough.

"I am not a botanist," said the Finn, considering the newcomer, "but I do believe that is a laurel branch in your hand?"

"It is indeed," smiled the visitor.

"Then you must be Apollo," concluded the folklorist, almost dizzy with all these encounters that in his mind proved once and for all that he had been right all along.

"Yes," answered the god considered brightest of all the Olympians.

Windy didn't waste any time. "So what does this thing do?" she asked, indicating the mechanism.

"I don't know," was the honest reply.

Suddenly, ADMIN fainted. His comrades rushed to help.

"What is all this blood?" asked PJ, realizing that ADMIN's pant leg was soaked.

"He must have gotten hit by the spear!" exclaimed Windy.

Hungry Gal was pissed off. "Why didn't he say anything?" They ripped the fabric open to reveal a deep gash on his thigh.

"I'll get a bandage," shouted the Kid, rushing towards the ladder.

"Look at that," said Manshin Mae in disbelief as the wound suddenly healed over completely, leaving no scar.

"I am sometimes called *the physician*," bragged Apollo.

"I had a dream," said ADMIN, regaining consciousness. "We were in a city, all of us. Protected by great walls. And by you too," he said to Apollo. "But it wasn't enough. Nothing could stop the enemy."

"That was Troy," said Apollo, with a tinge of melancholy. "You dreamt of Troy." He smiled with irony. "And, lo. Here we are once more."

That night, Club H made room to accommodate their new associates.

Bonghwang Rider was provided a bedroom on the top floor, right next to the entrance to the terrace: ADMIN had accurately surmised that easy access to the open air was the only way to entice her to stay. She mistrusted the entire household, disliking the fact that Haetae were "pack animals" as opposed to the glorious solitariness she experienced when she downloaded the mythical avian through her psyche and out into the world.

Once, a gumiho she had encountered nosing around a dolmen had told her in passing that she wasn't the only one of her kind. "So don't dip your feathers around here like you're somebody special," is what the creature had said, claiming that there was, in fact, a massive flock of bonghwang that had reminded the fox spirit of a cloud of flies—in her derogatory phrase—when she saw it at a distance. But since the number of hairs on a gumiho's nine tails was equal to the number of lies it told in one day, the bonghwang hostess didn't believe it for a second. Still, it bothered her. And did indeed make her question her uniqueness. Which was, of course, exactly what the fox had intended.

That night at the clubhouse, Bonghwang Rider dragged the floor mat out of the bedroom and onto the terrace and slept under the open sky. If she had any bad dreams or premonitions in this house of earth-pigs, she told herself, she would just fly away.

"The Mayor of Haetae Town says I can't be proven wrong," said Manshin Mae to Folklorist Halko in their guestroom overlooking the inner courtyard, recalling what ADMIN had stated during the battle outside the university.

Halko had been effusing about that moonlit enclosure all evening long. This was his first time in a hanok, and he declared it the perfect dwelling for a scholar, with the quadrangle below metaphorically representing the light inside the mind. The mudang was tired of listening to that sort of thing, and had hoped to start an argument and get him off the subject.

"But neither can I," he responded.

"Occam's Razor says otherwise."

"Enlighten me."

"Your explanation," she complied, "involving as it does, Imaginal worlds and real presences from alternate universes, requires that we rewrite what is known about how all of reality works. It is cosmological. While I stay in the realm of psychology only. My explanation is by way of Freud's idea of projection, Jung's archetypes and collective unconscious, with the addition of psychokinesis to move stuff around. I'm not thrilled about needing to invoke the latter, but so be it."

"That's still a lot of assumptions."

"A couple of orders of magnitude less than yours. And I don't leave the physical laws of the known universe behind." She indicated the lamp on the floor next to them. "I can't disprove a hypothesis claiming that trillions of tiny angels are flying out of the wall along that wire and singing a song to the filament in the bulb to get it to shine. But it's simpler to just say electrons."

Several seconds passed in silence, followed by Halko's sudden smile. "I like that very much."

"What?"

"Subatomic particles—"

"Don't say it—"

"Are all celestial beings."

"Hopeless."

Halko and Mae kissed each other goodnight, the mudang reached over and switched off the lamp, and they and the myriads of myriads of angels along the lamp wire were all instantly asleep.

⁂

That same night, Haenyeo Nam made room in her bed for the young woman she thought was her daughter. Aphrodite, like the others of her kind, rarely if ever had need of sleep. But here on this lovely island, so much like Kythera, the isle of her birth, with these women of the sea—and as all seas were precious to her, so were they— she slept like a baby. The gods did not dream unless dreaming was their purview, but on this night, Aphrodite dreamt of going to the mainland, being discovered by an agency at a café in Apgujeong, fast-tracked to stardom of one type or another, and hearing her name on more lips than had ever praised or prayed or pleaded desperately to her in the days of Athens and Sparta, Troy and Ithaca. When she woke in the morning, she was glad she had lived that other life only in a dream, happy to be here on a mat on the hard floor, ready to get ready for a day of diving into the sea.

On their way out to the ferry boat, Aphrodite spotted one of the island's famous hareubangs: a stone statue of a grandfather figure with a conical hat and hands held across its midsection. She immediately approached and bowed politely before it. "Uncle Poseidon," she petitioned, "please let the seas be calm today. We have a lot of work to do."

"Who knew," said a young man, stepping into view, "that my pretty sister would finally find her true calling hawking shellfish and overawing the locals with her smile?"

"Who knew," responded Aphrodite, "that my annoying little brother would show up unannounced to bother me when I most wanted to be unbothered? Me. I knew."

Hermes laughed. "I'll leave if you want me to. And won't say another word."

"About what?" asked Aphrodite, unable to suppress her curiosity and her instinct for gossip, an indulgence shared by all the Olympians.

"Athena and Apollo are at it again."

"At *what*?"

"Each other's throats," he answered. "I believe they intend to refight the Trojan War."

"Of course they do. Nobody ever just lets themselves enjoy." She indicated the simple surroundings.

"So whose side are you on?" he continued with a wicked look.

"Do you remember what happened the last time?" she asked. "*I hurt my hand.*" She held up her left hand. "In *battle*." Then she reconsidered—was it the left or the right?—and held up her right instead, indicating the wrist. "Look, I still have a scar."

Hermes took her hand and inspected it. "No, you don't."

"Of course I don't. The point is, I remember the pain. And I don't like pain. And stop trying to hold my hand."

"Be on *my* side."

"What are you talking about?"

"They messed around for ten years in Ilium, fighting each other by proxy, and all I did was run a few errands. This time, they're going to battle, one-on-one, to prove which of them is the best. I can feel it."

"So let them."

"But *I'm* the best."

She laughed. "The cutest, maybe. That's hardly the same."

"I'm the best. And I intend to prove it."

"What do you want me to do?"

"Support me or look away. But don't come in on either of their side."

"Can you see what I'm doing right now?" she asked.

"What are you talking about?"

"I'm looking away," she said, not looking at him.

She sold a bag of abalone to a gaggle of youngsters who had pooled their money just to approach her. "How adorable they are," she said to Hermes.

But he was already gone.

On the street in front of the hanok-style mansion, two life-sized Haetae statues seemed to have been installed to look like exact duplicates of the monuments in front of Gyeongbokgung Palace.

Then they *moved*.

And suddenly resumed the forms of their hosts: PJ and Hungry Gal.

"Do you think we can order delivery like this?" asked the latter.

"What do Haetae eat except fire?"

"A really crispy barbeque might work."

"You can try," encouraged PJ.

"I don't want to eat alone."

"We'll embarrass ourselves. Some goddess from a couple thousand years ago will attack and we've got barbeque sauce smeared all over our faces."

"Do you really think I care about that?"

"No."

"Right."

She lifted her phone and opened her delivery app.

On the rooftop terrace, another Haetae was on guard, pacing back and forth, as if taking the job seriously. A buzzing sound caught its attention: the smartphone resting on one of the small tables was vibrating.

The Haetae transformed and resumed the form of its human host: the Kid. He sighed at the interruption and checked the screen: it was Hungry Gal. "What," he answered.

"We're getting galbi. You in?"

"From where?"

"New place."

"I don't want to risk it."

"What's the problem?"

"Maybe it sucks."

"It's got good reviews."

"If it sucks and I'm still hungry—"

"Nobody feels your pain more than me, okay?" said Hungry Gal, and he knew she meant business.

"Okay." He set down the phone. And in a moment, had again transformed into a Haetae. It glanced up into the sky.

The bonghwang circled above, like a Nazgul.

The Haetae watched for a moment: Were the two creatures akin? Natural allies? Natural enemies? For the moment, at any rate, they seemed to be on the same side.

In the stone circle deep underground rested the Promethean mechanism. Windy sat alone, watching it. As the strongest of the hosts, she had agreed to be the last line of defense in case somebody came after it.

"Hey," she said, talking to the device as if it were a person, "don't pretend you can't hear me. I know you got everybody all excited, but I don't trust you. Nothing is free in the world. What do you want?"

There was no answer. But she didn't really expect one.

On the ferry ride out to the tiny island, the woman who called Aphrodite her daughter was chatting with the boat driver and his cronies, telling them all about how grateful she was now that they had been reunited. The men indulged her in this belief, because it was no skin off their noses to let somebody be happy for a moment or two in a world with so much pain.

"I'm an intangible cultural heritage, what the hell are you?" Haenyeo Pang said to Aphrodite, after the two of them had been silently staring at each other for several minutes.

"When first they saw me, the immortal gods raised their hands, praying, all of them, to take me home as their wedded wife, so dazzled they were with my coming, with my face, framed by a crown of violets."

The diver didn't quite know how to respond. So she spat over the side of the boat instead. "You are not her daughter," she finally said. "How dare you hurt her like that."

"You just don't like seeing her smile."

The woman's face went hot: it was too accurate an observation.

The two cousins made ready for the dive as they always did, pulling on their wetsuits and getting the float and diving line together and strapping on their weight belts. Just before they entered the sea, Haenyeo Nam told Aphrodite, "You can wait for us. Don't go into the water without me." Then the cousins swam away from the shore.

Aphrodite observed the tide pool for a while, and laughed at the antics of a small crab that appeared to be dancing for her benefit.

When the two haenyeo swam back a couple hours later with their catch, the young woman was nowhere to be seen.

"Where? Where? If I lose her again, I'll die. I'll die."

Haenyeo Pang took her at her word, and immediately went back out over the tide pool and dove as soon as the water was deep enough. Down she went, swimming quickly back and forth, seeing nothing, then went deeper. Until she saw something that made her think she had been under for too long: Aphrodite floated as if seated on a throne on the sea floor, with an open mesh sack. Sea snails and crabs and various crustaceans were crawling into it of their own desire, wanting only to be nearer to her.

Daydream or not, thought the haenyeo, as she swam deeper, took the young woman's hand and hauled her toward the surface.

When they reached the shore, Haenyeo Nam was so relieved she forgot to cry. Aphrodite showed her the full sack of sea urchins, conches and sea snails and the woman laughed with joy. But her cousin wasn't smiling.

ADMIN Yoon had introduced Apollo Lee to the clubhouse library, and they were looking up various ancient contraptions that might hold a clue to the function of the mechanism Windy was watching over in the basement. A book on archeology had large photographs of an ancient device that had been discovered in a sea wreck off the coast of Antikythera over a century before. It was not dissimilar in some respects from what they were investigating.

"This is an orrery," observed ADMIN.

"On first and even second glance," agreed Apollo. "But a third? Don't be so sure."

"What do you mean?"

"The most gifted of craftworkers sometimes disguise their greatest inventions by giving them two functions: that which is obvious and that which is not." He indicated the device in the photographs. "Those gears can be moved to track the proper timing of the Olympiad, even to predict the skies. But there may well have been a deeper purpose, something the authors of this book never anticipated. And now, because they have stopped looking, will never find."

ADMIN thought about that for a moment. Then stretched his leg.

"How is your wound?" asked Apollo.

"All better, thanks to you."

Apollo nodded a silent acknowledgment.

"I wonder, can you also heal something a bit worse?"

"The affliction in your blood?"

ADMIN was taken aback. He had revealed his cancer diagnosis to nobody, certainly not to this stranger professing to be an ancient deity. "Yes, the 'affliction' in my blood."

"I am a physician but I have my limitations as well."

"I understand."

"You are afraid?"

"Of death? Who is not? I don't look forward to the pain. The doctors have warned me about it."

"There is always hemlock."

"That's not my style," said ADMIN. He seemed suddenly sheepish but plowed ahead anyway. "I have read about your golden arrows, that Apollo is the archer who never misses his mark. In the *Odyssey*, there is a happy island with no sickness, and when someone grows old, it is said that you end their lives with a gentle arrow. It flies unseen and strikes without leaving a mark, delivering a painless death, as if drifting away in sleep."

"And you wonder," asked the god, "if I might do that for you?"

"Forgive me for the imposition."

Apollo just looked at him. "You have sung no paeans to me, you have not prayed my name aloud, you have never stood before my statue, even if headless and broken, and felt the awe in your brain become the words of the poet: *you must change your life.*"

"That would be idolatry," said ADMIN quietly.

"Of course it would," replied Apollo, not understanding why the very mechanism of ancient Greek religion would be something to avoid.

"I am a member of the Presbyterian Church. 'You will have no gods before me' is one of the rules."

"Well, then," replied the god of knowledge, healing, music, prophecy and, most relevant to the matter they were discussing, archery, "you are on your own."

Suddenly, there was a thundering BOOM outside that shook the foundations of the house. They both rushed to the window. Down below, Athena, goddess of war was pounding on a battle drum.

Across town, among a row of small, old, identical-looking warehouses along the Han River, Hermes had found a card game and could not seem to lose. The game was blackjack, the illegal casino was in one of the storerooms rented by Boss Kang.

The charming young Korean man who happened to be the Greek god of gambling paused for a moment to turn from the table and yank on the lever of one of the half dozen slot machines crammed onto the floor: jackpot!

He laughed, grabbed the winnings, and immediately placed them on the table, making another bet. He won that round too. Again, his laughter rang out. It was not a derisive bark or a victorious crowing: just the sound of delight. The other gamblers, hardened, bitter, angry at their own losses, could not help but smile, suddenly realizing that they too, were somehow having a good time.

But the Boss didn't share that sentiment. It was his money that this fun-loving young man was taking. He moved over to the blackjack table.

"How is it," he asked, loud enough to be heard by the whole room, "that you cannot seem to lose?"

Everybody stopped what they were doing to watch.

"I cheat," said Hermes.

Boss Kang could not believe his own ears. "What?"

"I'm a literal god of luck, but even luck needs a little help now and again."

The gangster barely had to tilt his head in a command gesture for several strong hands to grab hold of the brash young man and stop any possible escape on his part.

"You'll have to pay up," said Boss Kang. "And it's going to cost you a lot more than what you 'won.'"

"I have just the thing," replied Hermes. "But I need to run across town to get it."

Everybody laughed.

"You're kidding, right?" asked Kang.

Suddenly, Hermes *yawned*. "Sorry," he said, 'I'm not tired, really. And I'm certainly not bored." Again he yawned.

Several gamblers followed suit. In matter of moments, the whole place was trying to stifle the same. When even the Boss finally couldn't help himself, he realized that everybody had fallen asleep: in their chairs, even on their feet.

"See you soon," said Hermes.

And in one breath, Boss Kang too, had nodded off.

Apollo stood outside the entrance to the huge hanok, flanked by PJ and Hungry Gal in their Haetae forms: pacing back and forth like agitated lions, massive and menacing.

Athena was before him, the broken halves of her spear in each hand.

"You have something I want," she stated.

"Yes."

"My favorite in this city will put it to good use."

"I think she will not," predicted Apollo. "And I am the god of prophecy."

"An oracle can be mistaken," she countered. "It is my wise judgement that the device is best left to me and my chosen one. And I," she concluded with the closest she ever got to a smile, "am the goddess of wisdom."

"You broke your spear," he observed.

"Which you knew already."

"I was emphasizing the point, pardon the pun."

"To underline for me, that this polis, this place with its people and other... inhabitants"—she indicated the forbidding Haetae and the shrieking bonghwang circling overhead—"is unknown to us and therefore poses unexpected dangers. And so I should take my shattered lance as a warning sign. And let you do what you want to do."

"I supposed the conclusion does not exactly follow from the argument," he admitted.

"Correct. And so, despite the unknowns, I prefer to do what *I* want to do."

Suddenly, the ground rumbled beneath them, and when Athena glanced up, the hanok had been lifted dozens of meters into the air by thick walls that had pushed up from the foundation. The sight was dizzying, dreamlike, yet hard as stone.

"I once built the walls of Troy," said Apollo. "These too, will hold."

"Just you and me," countered Athena. "Right here. Or any place else. My spear is broken. I am at a disadvantage—"

With blinding speed, she had raised the sharp end of the broken weapon to Apollo's throat. But too quickly to perceive, he held a golden arrow at her own.

It was a standoff.

"Not bad, for a singer," said Athena.

A loud snore interrupted the moment. They could not help but lower their weapons and turn in the direction of the sound: both of the huge Haetae were asleep behind them. And on the rooftop above, the bonghwang's long neck was dangling over the edge of the terrace, its head lolling in slumber.

"*Hermes*," said both the gods at once, alarmed and annoyed.

Apollo suddenly made his eyes distant and farseeing. In his mind's gaze, he quickly roamed the rooms of the clubhouse, descended into the ancient ground of the basement, and saw Windy fast asleep. The mechanism that Prometheus had stolen from the workshop of Olympus was nowhere to be seen.

"It is too late," he said. "The prize is gone."

"Where?" she said, angered.

"I don't know. He has wrapped himself in a cloud."

A small cumulus drifted through the gambling den across town, and each sleeping gambler that it passed by was roused awake. It finally came to rest in the same place Hermes had last been standing and he reappeared out of the dissolving mist, the purloined, immortal mechanism in his hands.

The Boss regained consciousness and was surprised at what he saw.

"Are we even?" asked Hermes Lee, handing the device over to Boss Kang, who could not help but take it in both hands. And as he did, the metallic surface shimmered, as if some power within was waking up.

"The Boss suddenly remembered a story he had heard his grandmother tell, about a nine-tailed fox that kept a jewel under its tongue. If a man could snatch the jewel and put it in his own mouth, and the first thing he saw was the sky, then he would know the workings of Heaven, but if instead he first looked down, he would know everything there was to know about Earth. His grandmother had explained that the moral of the story was to look up and not down, to follow Heaven and not the world. But even as a boy, Kang had said to himself: 'Who cares about what goes on in Heaven? Everything I want is right in front of me.' And so it was that the grown man thought the same."

Boss Kang turned to the gamblers who filled his illegal operation. "Go home, friends. We're closed for the night." Some grumbled, some were relieved, but they all headed out the doors. And when they were gone, only a handful of his soldiers remained, along with the charming young man whose activities had upended the evening. That and the strange, volleyball-sized mechanism now in the Boss's hands.

"What does it do?" he asked.

"I have a feeling that's up to you," answered Hermes.

At a small chueotang restaurant several blocks from Seoul Station—where the older, narrower streets had "scheduled for demolition" scrawled on the walls outside a few of the small shops that lined them—Zeus Lee had found a place that suited his mood. The thick, salty soup made from practically an entire school of ground, tiny loach fish was considered a fortifier of the libido—which he did not need, despite his nonstop activities in that regard—and a super-releaser, as they say in ethology, of melancholy, memory, and regret, of which, being an immortal, he had a surplus.

An older man who wore an eyepatch and was seated across from him had started that particular ball rolling a short while before, by reminiscing about how hard his father had treated him and his siblings. It had been just after the war, food was scarce, everybody had to do everything possible for the family to survive. "But did that excuse the beatings?" he asked rhetorically, as the steam from the soup followed the path of least resistance upward and around his craggy features. "I still have the scars."

"Scars?" chimed in another old gentleman with a walking stick seated at the god's side. "I still feel the pain in my bones. Anything above thirty percent humidity, and my legs ache from where my father hit us."

The other diners considered those onerous details, lost in their own memories.

"My father *ate* all my brothers and sisters," said Zeus Lee, "swallowed them whole. After I was born, he tried to do the same to me but my mother hid a rock in my swaddle and he downed that instead. The old monster."

He stopped talking but the others clearly wanted to hear more. "And?" "Yes?" "So?"

"And yes, so I grew to maturity, poisoned my father, and made him puke up my siblings. Then we went to war against him and his old cronies. And finally destroyed them. After ten long years."

Nobody knew what to say. The big man considered all of them. "Had you been at my side, it would have taken ten minutes."

Everybody in the restaurant cheered.

"The veil, speaking poetic like, between the universes was getting thinner. I was seeing Haetae chasing after busses for fun, and the new girl's bonghwang flying overhead almost everywhere we happened to be. At that point I could jump into a Haetae pretty much any time I wanted—or vice versa, depending on how this all works. So I had to wonder..."

"Could I take your big chicken for a spin around the block?"

"She's not mine and she'd be really annoyed that you called her that."

Windy Lee and Bonghwang Rider—who turned out to be a Kim when ADMIN finally inquired, as Windy hadn't bothered to ask her name—were on the rooftop terrace of the mansion that Club Haetae called home. The huge bonghwang flew slow circles above them, like a hawk after a meal keeping an active search pattern for a mouse on the ground below out of habit rather than hunger.

"Didn't mean anything personal. How would I go about it?"

"Just jump off the roof. If she likes you, then you'll merge. If not, nice knowing you. Sort of."

"You're kidding."

"Yeah."

"Really."

"You *really* want to do it?"

"Of course. "

"I'll ask."

"Me too," said Windy.

" 'Me too' what?"

"Don't you want to try being a Haetae?"

"And stay on the ground?"

"They can jump pretty high. It's practically flying."

"Not my style."

So Ms. Kim asked and the bird said, Sure why not? In so many words.

Windy-as-bonghwang flew over Mapo Bridge, experiencing both the ancient exhilaration of flight—the sense of freedom bundled with a new set of limitations to be negotiated—and an unexpected surge of compassion for any jumpers, overcome by the details of their lives or brain chemistry, who might be leaping even now to their intended deaths off the span below.

Windy had always thought of herself as lacking in empathy, so the strong sense of concern for a potentially distraught stranger struck her as originating from the mythological creature she was hosting rather than from her own nature. It made some sense that while the Haetae seemed to possess the ironlike ability to discern good from bad—like a righteous Confucian magistrate—the bonghwang, centuries-old symbol of idealized royalty, would seem much more magnanimous. And so she, too, felt that sense of protectiveness over the beings who in this case were not just figuratively but literally below her, way down there on the ground.

That made her wonder if the feelings she experienced as a result of hosting the Haetae—the sense of family, of friendship, of belonging—were not her at all, but the Haetae. And if that were true then maybe every feeling and emotion were also not her at all, but came from some passing deity or spirit she happened to be unknowingly hosting at that particular moment.

Her bonghwang vision picked up nothing unhappy happening on the bridge, and so she turned and followed the Han westward, coursing along its northern edge, until her keen gaze discerned, poking out of the water below, a dozen massive heads—as though a herd of hippos were plowing through the shallow water of the riverbank.

What in the world?

She pulled in her wide wings and dove for a closer look: it was the Haetae swimming as if they were following after her. Maybe they had reason to be irritated or jealous about Windy moonlighting as host to a harpy, as it were. But that wasn't the mood: they were just having a good time at the river, like so many other Seoulites.

Windy smiled, though on the face of the huge avian it looked like little more than a slightly twisted beak. Don't worry guys, she thought, charmed by the sight of them. I miss my pack too much to do too much more of this.

Then she dove straight down and, just as it seemed like she would smash into the lead Haetae, pulled up out of the dive and dropped out of the bonghwang itself and into the pack leader, suddenly seeing no longer through the eyes of the great bird but through those of the Haetae.

"I was shocked by how easy it was: to go from monster to monster like hopping from one stepping stone to the next."

At the emptied gambling den, Boss Kang and his apparent accomplice, the Greek god whose various appellations included watcher-near-the-door, presider-at-the-race-track, easy-going-and-friendliest but also full-of-multiple-wiles and most-deceitful-to-gods-and-humans, had been turning, twisting, bouncing and even kicking at the mysterious mechanism with no further indication of function beyond the deep hum that had occurred when the mobster first took it in hand.

"Surely, we are almost there," encouraged Hermes.

But Kang was not so sure: not about the device and not about the young man whose charm was wearing thin.

"Boss!" shouted a man who had just rushed up the stairs, "We're being hit!" The blood on his scalp testified to the truth of his declaration.

The god of thieves attracted his followers to wherever he went, and the Boss's warehouse casino, no matter how hidden and well guarded, was no exception. "My fault," admitted Hermes.

But before he could explain, the shouting and fighting down below overwhelmed all other considerations.

"How many?" asked the Boss.

"Twenty!" shouted one of his men.

That was ten more than they could probably handle. It was no doubt Boss Jeong, who would not leave well enough alone, despite Boss Kang's great efforts at making no waves and being as peaceable as possible given the industry they all worked in.

"If only we had guns," complained Kang, setting the device down on a table and thinking of his counterparts in the USA, who all would have been armed. Korean policies had left him and his kind with nothing but bare hands, baseball bats and on very serious occasions, fish-gutting knives. Which meant that being seriously outnumbered, as he was right now, was not something mere toughness could overcome. "If we only had guns."

The mechanism on the table shimmered: the light around it started to coalesce into matter. Gradually, layer after layer, as the seconds passed, a dozen shapes came into view, first transparent, then finally becoming opaque, solid, recognizable objects: 9mm semiautomatic pistols.

"Well, look at that," said Hermes, as surprised as the rest. "What are they?"

The Boss quickly grabbed one of the weapons and gave it a closer look. "Loaded," he confirmed. Then quickly waved his soldiers over, who armed themselves not quite believing what they had just seen. One of them was Blue Wolf, the young thug whose arm Windy had bitten off on the subway. It had been replaced with a prosthetic, which did not seem to have slowed down the would-be fierce warrior at all. He grabbed one of the guns expertly in his remaining hand.

As he and the other men rushed down the stairs and into the fray, Boss Kang glanced at Hermes then looked again at the mechanism.

"How about a rocket launcher?" he asked.

The device hummed and the photons around it started to take shape. As an experiment, the mobster waved his hand through the coalescing RPG-7: it went right through the gathering particles of light.

"I think this one might take a little longer," suggested Hermes.

The battle on the warehouse grounds was still furious, despite the sudden appearance of the handguns. The lack of familiarly with firearms made the Boss' staff less effective than they might otherwise had been. Three of the weapons were wrested from them in close fighting, and now everybody was shooting at each other, taking cover behind the big shipping containers scattered across the asphalt. It was a loud, violent stalemate.

Then Boss Kang arrived with his newly birthed antiartillery weapon and fired a rocket that blasted the metal container next to the rival gangsters. It blew up in a massive explosion: the container was filled with a cargo of highly flammable herbicide intended for shipment off the books. The attackers instantly fled the scene, and Kang watched with satisfaction that soon turned to concern as the fiery debris from the explosion landed all around the grounds—and kept burning.

Windy & Company had appeared on the scene even before the rocket launcher materialized, led there the old-fashioned way: by one of their number—this time it was Kid Kee—taking off across town in a fugue state. They had gotten used to invoking the Haetae at will in the wake of the detonation of the Titan that had weakened the barrier between the worlds. So when the Kid's eyes suddenly glazed over in the middle of dinner, they were almost surprised.

"Don't we have bigger fish to fry?" asked Hungry Gal, annoyed at the interruption.

Regardless, they followed where the Kid led, and ended up at a row of cheap warehouses along the river in the middle of an apparent war between gangs.

Then a shoulder rocket blew the place up and the Kid had to put out the fire.

Firetrucks and police cars were quickly on the scene, and as always of late, everybody was baffled to find the flames already gone. But the cops were here to bust up a turf war and so they arrested gang members from both sides. A police detective spotted Boss Kang and moved to grab him but Hermes was quicker: the god of clean getaways threw a cloud around the two of them and walked right through the center of the action to the nearest street, where Kang hailed a cab that got them out of there.

Blue Wolf recognized Windy immediately. He moved quickly toward her, raising his gun. Then, close enough to fire, he shouted one word at her, wanting her to recognize him. "Freak."

She glanced up, with no idea who he was, but the momentarily delay was enough. The moment Blue Wolf pulled the trigger a wheelchair smashed into him and threw off his aim enough for the bullet to miss its target.

Law enforcement converged on him; Windy was shaken up by the close call. Arson Investigator Kim steadied his chair and moved over to her. "Are you alright?"

"You saved my life," she said in answer.

"Then we're even."

She didn't know what he was talking about.

At a daepojip—an old meat shop with circular, metal-covered tables that had holes cut out of their middles for a center grill—Arson Investigator Kim cooked the beef for himself and his guest, Windy Lee. Rather than standing as was her custom with anybody she didn't know, Windy found herself seated across from him without a second thought. As if she had known the man forever. Then he seemed to confirm it.

"It's been a very long time," he said.

"A few weeks," she responded, mystified, recalling that his interrogation of her and PJ was fairly recent.

"Actually, more like twenty-five years." When she didn't say anything, he continued. "It was you who put out the blaze at the officetel in Seochon. You were one year old. I was trying to reach you but the corner of the building collapsed. Turned out the contractors skimped on the materials in the superstructure. But that's beside the point. I was pinned down under a pile of badly made concrete. The fire was coming for me." He thought for a moment. "It's like a living thing, you know?"

"I know," Windy said quietly.

"It talks to you, when you're in the middle of it. And it was talking a blue streak. Wouldn't shut up, in fact. Saying how bad the next couple of minutes were going to be for me. At least, that's what I imagined. I was terrified. All my training went out the window. I just waited to die. And then."

Suddenly, the charcoal in the bin under their table sputtered out. Smoke fumes came out the side vents and the restaurant staff rushed over to fix the situation, apologizing profusely.

"Well," smiled Kim, indicating the sputtering grill, "that's what happened. The fire was gone. And I was still there."

A long moment between them.

"Thank you for trying to save me," said Windy. "I'm sorry."

"That I'm in this chair? I'm not. I'm *alive*."

The charcoal was going again, and Arson Investigator Kim went back to cooking.

"Thanks to you."

"Not me. The Haetae."

"I thought you might say that."

"Is that why I'm being interrogated at a meat joint instead of your office?"

"I thought you might be more forthcoming without audio recorders and CCTV."

"I see."

They both ate for a bit. In fact, the BBQ tasted so good that they continued to eat for a long while, in silence, until they were finished.

Then Windy cut loose. "My friend believed what your arsonist had to say: about the coming stage in human evolution, about contacting the universe next door, freeing an advanced being named Prometheus and being rewarded by some fancy technology that would make everything that had come before it seem"—she struggled to find the words, not accustomed to talking like this—"*less* fancy. And it was all true. I mean it worked. My friend really did those things. But there was a big negative reaction you could say, which my friend also expected might happen. And so I got involved to nip it in the bud. Or at least, the Haetae did. And when it was all over, I had some kind of magical device in my hands."

A long moment.

"You left out the big bird."

"You *saw* that?"

"I saw something. Like I was daydreaming. But it wasn't my imagination."

"Yeah, the bonghwang showed up. And then a bunch of Greek gods. Because the event made the fabric between the universes more permeable." Windy thought for a second and then clarified. "I mean the bird was already here. She lives in Seoul. The guys out of Greece are new."

"And your 'friend'? Somebody you're in love with?"

"Yes." Windy was caught off guard by the question and surprised to have answered it the way she did.

"It happens."

"Not to me it doesn't."

"Is he okay?"

"He disappeared. Maybe in the fire that I put out. Maybe he was already gone. I don't know."

"I can try to help you find him if you want."

Windy was touched by the offer. "That's really nice of you to say. But I don't think he can be found. Not in this world."

They were silent for a moment.

"How is it all going to end?" asked Kim. "Speculate, please."

"I think maybe in something more than the Haetae can handle," answered Windy.

The no trespassing tape across the front of the construction site of the Tower of Olympus—the completion of which had been put on hiatus after the scandalous death of the CEO of the building's backer and the strange fire that had broken out momentarily on the top floor—had, warning aside, been trespassed. As a deity of borders, boundaries and crossroads, not to mention gateways, doorway, and even hinges, Hermes Lee was not to be put off by a strip of thin plastic. In fact, he gleefully added it to his list of honorifics: "tape jumper."

He guided Boss Kang onto the property and up the dizzying, exposed construction lift onto the summit. At that point, Hermes indicated the elevator they had just stepped away from. "Best if there is no way to follow us."

"That means no way down," said the Boss.

"Correct."

"Let's do it."

Hermes picked up a large and heavy wrench that had been left behind with a smattering of other construction tools, and moved back to the elevator.

"Can't you just wave a wand or something?" asked the career criminal.

"Here is the wand," said Hermes, regarding the wrench. He smashed the lift mechanism and hit the descend button: the elevator jammed and broke with a grinding sound. "That was the wave."

"Works for me."

They both couldn't help but consider the entire city before them: Hermes with aesthetic appreciation, Boss Kang with fantasies of ownership.

"Let's get started," said Hermes.

Kang opened the satchel he was carrying, revealing the mechanism that had converted photons to matter. And not just any matter, but advanced weaponry. Now they would see how far that could be taken.

"Go ahead," said Hermes, "as it seems to like you."

Indeed the device had responded to nobody else but the gangster, as if imprinted on him like a baby duck, if a baby duck could create a shoulder rocket out of thin air.

Boss Kang considered it for a moment. "I want," he said, "the most powerful weapon you can make."

The device hummed. Then spoke for the first time.

"What color?" it asked.

On the ferryboat ride back to Jeju, Haenyeo Pang waited until her cousin had stepped away for a moment to chat with the men in the wheelhouse as was her routine.

"Go home," whispered Haenyeo Pang with great intensity. "Go back to the Dragon King's Palace. Leave us alone. I hate that you are here."

"The only thing I hate are those who deny the power of love," responded Aphrodite, not caring if anyone overheard. "Who think they are somehow greater than it is, or somehow beyond its reach." She indicated the ferry boat driver. "That man over there, for instance."

"He's an ugly old fool," the diver interrupted.

"Has loved you since you were both children."

"He was an ugly young fool once."

"And you were too good for him."

"I was too good for anybody.

"A pretty thing. Yes, I can see that."

"You pretend to see a lot of things."

"But is he really as unappealing to you as you say?" wondered Aphrodite. "Look at the curvature of his arms, the small of his back, the flame in his eyes."

His arms sagged, his back was anything but small, but as she spoke the words, he turned to look at his old crush and his eyes seemed to shine.

"It's hard to believe you would not be head over heels in love," concluded the goddess.

"Well, believe it."

That night, Haenyeo Pang saw the newcomer asleep, head resting on her cousin's shoulder, as if indeed, they were mother and daughter. And she wondered, is it possible? A thought she instantly rejected.

But still, she could not sleep. The diver got up, pulled on a light coat and went outside for a walk. A few minutes later, she saw the ferryboat operator standing against a low wall, smoking, staring at the stars. He was startled to see her.

"You're always out here," she said. "Why is that?"

"It took you fifty years to ask me?"

"Yes."

"I remember the first time I came out here I had a very romantic explanation to impress you with. What I was doing out here alone, looking at the stars."

"What was it?"

"I don't recall."

"Really?"

"Yes. Because the whole plan was that you would not be able to sleep since you were thinking about me like I was thinking about you, and you would go for a walk and see me here and ask what I was doing and my story would make you love me even more. But since you slept like a rock for fifty years, I forgot what I was going to say."

The diver laughed and sat down next to him. "Make something up."

"I'm too old for that."

"Try."

"Can't do it on command. It's going to take a few nights."

"No rush." She suddenly rested her head on his shoulder. The ferryboat man couldn't believe it. His dream had come true after half a century.

" 'I'm waiting for a falling star.' " he admitted. "That's what I was going to say. And I was hoping you would say,

'Let's wait together.' "

Suddenly, there was a shooting star. They both laughed, delighted.

Back at the house, Aphrodite's eyes were open. She was looking out the window at the same falling star. She tilted her head and in response another meteor flashed across the sky.

Apollo Lee sat in the library of the hanok-styled clubhouse, deep in contemplation. In his far-ranging mind, he reached across the skyline of Seoul and onto its surfaces and into its depths—the avenues, the alleys, the underground malls and the Metro tunnels—all in the attempt to find some clue as to the location of his troublesome little brother.

At last, he felt a "hit" or at the very least, that he was getting warmer.

He exited the library, moved through the wood-paneled corridors to the media room, and stepped inside. "I have pierced the cloud in which Hermes has hidden himself. Partially. I believe he is in the northern quadrant of the city."

The entire household, visitors included, were in front of the TV monitor, watching the news, which showed an immense hoplite coming into view in the middle of Jongno.

The newscaster provided the details. "What a difference a day makes. Only yesterday, Vice President of Operations Lim at the beleaguered Titanis Corporation refused to answer questions from reporters about the death of CEO Kan or the status of its partially completed, megatall skyscraper known as the Tower of Olympus. But today, that same building is the site of the largest holographic projection ever attempted: an ancient Greek warrior six hundred meters tall, from sandals to helm..."

"I think you got scooped," PJ said to Apollo, who watched in stunned surprise.

"A PR stunt," continued the newscaster, "clearly designed to tell the world that Titanis Corporation is alive and well and still in the game of high technology."

"That is no 'stunt,'" said the god. "That is Talos taking form. When he is complete, there will be nothing in your world that can stop him."

Across town, Athena Lee was telling VP Lim the same thing, as they watched the same news program. "Talos was a giant automaton invented by Hephaestus, destroyed by Jason and Medea. It appears that the immortal blacksmith's design still exists."

The top floor of the megastructure had begun to resemble the inside of a gigantic, hollow head. Boss Kang and his otherworldly helper stared downward from one of the two immense eye openings at the same monumental figure's body taking shape below them. But from their vantage, it was obvious this was not a holographic projection: the mysterious mechanism stolen by Prometheus was, in fact, constructing this apparently brazen warrior of solid matter from the outside in, like a gargantuan 3D printer.

"I was hoping for something a little more portable," observed Boss Kang. He turned away from the vertiginous view. "And easier to hide."

"Once Talos is completed, what need is there to hide?" asked Hermes. "These are strata of adamantine, the metal of the gods, that your little machine is layering one atop the next. There is nothing that can penetrate it. Not in this universe."

"It looks like Taekwon V," said the Boss, referring to the classic giant robot series.

"Is that a local hero?"

"Yes," answered Kang, not wanting to explain all the

details to this young man who looked Korean but seemed in many ways like a foreigner.

"In any case, Talos will be yours to control." Hermes indicated the command chair, which looked like an ancient marble throne, that was taking shape in the middle of the room. "A single demonstration of its power and you can bend the world to your will."

"They'll come after us before it's finished."

"Without effect," said the deity. "As thin as the matter still is at this point, it is enough to keep out even Apollo and Athena—the only forces in your world that might conceivably stop it from being completed. Since Zeus appears to be sitting this one out."

"Who are they?"

Hermes was saddened by that question, as he was by his own anonymity on twenty-first century Earth. "My half-brother and half-sister and father."

"Interesting family."

"To put it mildly."

"What's in all this for you?" the Boss asked.

Hermes considered for a moment. And decided honesty, as much as he despised it, was not going to work against him. "I'm respected enough, where I'm from. But for once, I want more. I want to be *feared*. I want to be looked upon with *awe*."

Boss Kang suddenly felt a kinship with the strange young man, whose startling arrival and life-changing instigations he had just gone along with because it all seemed to be working to his advantage. But this was different. He knew this desire, because it had gnawed at him his entire life. "Same, same," he said.

Hermes felt encouraged, his tongue loosening in a way it never would have among fellow immortals let alone a creature whose life by comparison lasted about as long as one beat of a sparrow's wing.

"I was born into a powerful family," he confided. "Everybody looked up to us—literally and otherwise. I was considered the friendly one. The guy you call upon for a tip before you bet on the races. Not the one whose name you cry out when there's nobody else to turn to: when you're in love but spurned or you want to have a baby but cannot or before you go into combat or you are old and sick and dying. My father and mother, my sisters and brothers get those... petitions. Not me." He almost said "prayers" and caught himself at the last moment. But Hermes need not have bothered: his audience had already been won over.

Boss Kang indicated an imaginary vista before them, spoke as if he were a tourist guide. "See that hole in the ground two blocks across? Boss Kang stomped his foot.

See how Namsan Mountain is over there now? Boss Lee moved it."

Hermes suddenly felt something that gods as a rule never feel: gratitude.

Apollo and Athena arrived at the literal foot of the immense Greek hoplite—even the sandal towered above them.

Taking aim at the giant's chest plate far above, Athena flung the pointed half of her spear, while her half-brother shot his golden arrows over and over again.

Their missiles all stuck into the massive chest. It could be penetrated after all.

But before they could celebrate this indication of vulnerability in the target, the adamantine formed another layer just beneath where the weapons had struck, and they popped out and fell back through the air, landing on the street where Apollo and Athena stood.

Athena grabbed her spear and leapt, jamming the point into the exposed foot of the giant; it didn't leave a mark.

"Try the aegis," suggested Apollo.

Even before the words were out of his mouth, Athena had tapped the image of the medusa on her Versace t-shirt. In response, it let out a roaring sound that escalated until even the two gods had to cover their ears. And when it ended, Talos had not even taken notice.

"I don't believe even the thunderbolt of Zeus could make an impression," said Apollo. "Even if he were not on *holiday*."

"I have the keys to the chest that keeps the thunderbolt," said Athena.

"I was not going to be so bold as to suggest that you use it without permission. But since our father is apparently unreachable..."

Athena stuck the halves of her spear into her belt, and took up a solid stance on the street, then closed her eyes in concentration.

In a few seconds, Apollo watched as dark storm clouds suddenly gathered directly above them.

Zeus sat on the concrete patio outside a CU convenience mart with his two new friends, the two ajusshi from the chueotang restaurant a few nights previously. They were drinking soju and eating tuna right from the can—as though they had known each other for decades.

Even from here, the gargantuan Talos figure taking shape could be seen, like a colossus looming above the city.

A thundercloud had gathered out of nowhere, just above the summit, and lightning was crashing over and over again against the helm of the huge warrior that everybody in the city had assumed was a holographic projection.

Zeus glanced once and sighed. Annoyed.

"What's wrong, friend?" said Walking Stick.

"Gave my daughter the keys to the car," complained Zeus speaking figuratively. "Just wish she'd tell me before she went for a drive."

"Kids," said Eyepatch.

"What can you do?" agreed Walking Stick.

"What if *I* wanted to use it?" continued Zeus.

"Exactly," agreed Eyepatch.

"No consideration," chimed in Walking Stick.

"Well," said Zeus regretfully, pushing away from the table. "I'd better go and check things out."

His companions glanced at each other, then back to Zeus.

"Can't let you do that," said Walking Stick.

Zeus looked at him, not yet angry. Just puzzled.

"Why not?"

"We enjoy your company too much," said Eyepatch, holding up the big keychain he always had on the table in front of him. Zeus saw that the keys were attached to a ring that dangled from a curious-looking baton: a miniature likeness of a "caveman" club with raised bumps on it. Eyepatch set the tiny club swinging back and forth. Zeus watched, momentarily entranced. Then tried to stand up from the table.

He couldn't move.

His two companions were dokkaebi.

Zeus may have been the King of the Gods in Olympus, but the goblins were on their home turf.

Another gentle swing of the keychain, and Zeus felt himself released of the magical hold. He relaxed in his chair, knowing there was no way to fight this.

"How many children do you have?" Walking Stick continued the conversation as if his shocking display of power had not just happened.

"Two hundred? A thousand? To be honest," answered Zeus, "I've lost count."

The two across the table studied him for a moment.

"He's telling the truth!" exclaimed Walking Stick, laughing.

Eyepatch looked at Zeus with genuine affection. "You're the best."

Zeus smiled back at them. And wondered how he was going to get out of this "friendship."

Watching the thunderstorm from inside the head of Talos, Boss Kang was unconcerned. "I was in an airplane hit by lightning once. It's no big deal."

"That is not lightning," said Hermes, amazed. "It's meant to *look* like lightning, for the benefit of the Bronze Age civilization over which it first appeared, and by that, I mean the ancient Greeks. But it is actually composed of much different material, an energy derived from cosmic sources and quite... invincible. That Talos does not even seem to notice is, well, notable."

Everybody at Club H had watched from the rooftop terrace as the lightning bolts struck the Talos figure with no visible effect on the image of the gigantic warrior and then, finally, just seemed to stop trying. The dark thundercloud dispersed in a matter of seconds.

"Maybe we all should bring over the Haetae and have the Haetae bite his ankles?" suggested Hungry Gal, to little enthusiasm.

"I think I have a way to defeat this apparition," said Folklorist Halko quietly. "To send these deities foreign to your land back where they came from. And to set everything right again."

Manshin Mae translated his English for the others.

"But I would hope," continued the folklorist, "that I might ask for something in return."

The gangster indicated the throne-like pilot's chair that was still taking form in the middle of the giant automaton's head. "I'm gonna try it out for size."

"Please do," encouraged Hermes.

Kang sat down on it and was immediately surrounded by bronze-punk, so to speak, interfaces: eyepieces and hand and leg controls seemingly composed of combinations of marble, bronze, leather and limestone. He peered through the crystalline eyepieces, and felt himself able to see not just all the way across Seoul, but across the Korean peninsula as well.

"That's not a bad view," he said, with his typical understatement.

"Try to lift one of the arms."

Kang moved his right hand. No reaction. "It's not doing anything."

"Just move one finger."

The Boss tried it; suddenly, there was a tremor throughout the room. And outside, Apollo and Athena standing below and the news helicopter flying above, all saw a twenty-five-meter-long index finger move up and down.

"It worked," said Boss Kang.

"Wonderful," exclaimed Hermes. "At this rate of manifestation, it appears Talos will be fully functional within a day's time. At which point..."

"I will take him for a walk," said Kang, "across town, across the country... I'm assuming bodies of water can't stand in its way?"

"No river or even sea," replied Hermes. "And I might imagine, since it is being manifested to fulfil a need in your world with its limitations and opportunities, that Talos can also *fly*. Given the right circumstances."

Boss Kang thought about all this, then indicated the mechanism that was humming along, building the gargantuan armored soldier. "I asked for a weapon. But I might have asked for something else. Anything else. Like enough food to feed everybody in the world. And the machine would have done it. Right?"

Hermes reacted, not wanting to encourage that unselfish train of thought, but once again, not wanting to be dishonest with his new partner, surprising even himself, as Hermes otherwise reveled in any opportunity to misguide or even lie outright. "Yes," he said simply.

"If I was the kind of person to wish for that," the gangster speculated, "then it would have been my first thought, not my last. People can't be what they are not," he concluded, referring to himself.

"On the contrary, in my experience people quite often become *exactly* what they are not," said Hermes. "That is one of the enduring charms of humanity." Hermes seemed almost to be hoping for a change in heart on the part of his partner in crime, making him a partner in some other, more compassionate endeavor. But that was not to come to pass.

"I guess," said Boss Kang, considering the evolving apparatus of conflict taking shape around him, "that ship has sailed."

Hermes smiled, but he could not reply, even though he wanted to. Something was wrong. And Kang could see it. Hermes stood frozen, eyes open but glazed over. He finally managed move his tongue. "There is a difference," he croaked, "between being invoked…"

"… and being kidnapped." The words were spoken by Manshin Mae, who was performing a gut on the terrace rooftop of Club H, accompanied by her elderly musicians, who had been brought over for the occasion.

Offerings of ouzo and stuffed grape leaves and olive oil had been set out in place of the usual rice cakes. Depictions in the history of art and popular culture of the Greek god Hermes had been found on the internet and printed out on the printer down in the library. They were stuck up on every surface where they could be seen by the mudang in the midst of her dancing invocation, that was, as the god himself pointed out, more like a summoning.

Folklorist Halko had stated his heart's desire: to visit his mother in Tuonela, the Finnish Land of the Dead. And the members of Club H, sympathetic but also seeing no other way to win his cooperation and hear his supposed solution to the destructive power that was taking shape in the center of Seoul, had agreed.

The first step: they needed a guide. Hermes, whose primordial task had always been to escort the Greek dead into Hades, was the perfect solution. But as he was busy trying to take over the world, they could not just *ask* him. Abduction was the only means of securing his cooperation. And that meant a gut by Manshin Mae that had whisked him from the inside of the monstrous Talos and held him without bail, more or less, inside the confines of her own head.

"You do know who you are messing with?" The words came from the mudang's lips, in her own voice, but with Hermes' personality and presence.

"We do," said ADMIN. "But prefer to present it to you

as an opportunity."

"This had better be irresistible," came the response.

Once, in a land that never saw a smoking tiger as no tiger ever wanted to be that cold, two Koreans went to Hell and back. Tuonela, the island of the dead in Finnish mythology, Folkorist Halko had explained to us, was extremely difficult to enter, as it was surrounded by nine seas and three forests and a black river, with passage only by way of a ferryboat operated by the daughter of Tuoni, the Lord of Death—unless, of course, one was already dead, in which case, it was impossible not to enter into Tuonela.

A great black swan swam those dark waters, and its song was bittersweet and nostalgic—a kind of send-off to the recently deceased, as if they didn't have enough mixed feelings to deal with. Many were the Finnish folktales about a powerful shaman hoping to level up who would attempt the trip to Tuonela in search of magic spells and so forth, whose first task was to convince the ferryboat gal that he was indeed dead.

Three of us had no hope of pretending we were dead, so the plan was for me to take the bonghwang as far as the river with Folklorist Halko and Manshin Mae on my back. Hermes was inside the mudang and so he was to be our guide. A couple thousand years ago, one of his main jobs had been guiding the dead to the Underworld of Greek mythology, so he jumped at the challenge of sneaking us into the Finnish Land of the Dead. He also was master of deception and disguises, so when we reached the river, he waved a little wand and suddenly I looked like a big black swan. We waited until the real big black swan disappeared around a bend in the river, then I flew straight over the water toward the island of the dead, in the hope that the daughter of the Lord of Death would just think 'Oh, there goes that big black swan I've seen every day for a gazillion years' if she even gave it that much thought. I didn't know any Finnish let alone Finnish songs, so I just sang my go-to karaoke number 'Magic Castle,' the one that says, 'In my dreams you are a princess under a spell, I promise I'll save you, no matter what, Past the magic castle and over the mire, now hold my hand, can you feel us rising? High in the sky, don't be scared, we're together.'

It wasn't my voice that came out, even if it was my intention. Who knew bonghwang could sing so sweetly?

"It worked. Because even in Hell, K-pop is irresistible."

A small house of pinewood could be seen in the distance, the only thing other than the expanse of white snow below them.

"That is it," said Halko.

The swan that was the bonghwang that was Windy Lee folded its wings and dropped altitude, coming in for a landing right in front of what turned out to be a pleasant little home, smelling of pine needles and salmon soup.

The great bird vanished, leaving Windy, Halko, and the mudang standing on the snow.

"As houses of the dead go," observed Manshin Mae in Hermes' voice, "this is downright cute."

"Could you be a little more... sensitive?" said Windy.

But Halko hadn't noticed. He was staring at the door of the small house, suddenly losing his courage. Then he realized the door was already open.

"Matthias."

He turned at the musical sound of his mother's voice. A voice he had not heard in thirty years. Not since the day she died. The only change in her appearance was her apparent health, which in death, had returned to her. Her eyes shone and her complexion was pink. She had spring flowers in her hair, despite being surrounded by eternal winter.

"Mother," was all he could say.

"My little boy."

Halko couldn't talk, he just wept.

"Did you come all this way to say you love me?" asked his mother.

He nodded his head and kept crying.

"You thought I didn't know?"

Again he could only nod. She opened her arms and he went to her and she held him.

"My sweet baby boy."

Having seen all this, Windy too, was crying, without making any attempt to stop herself.

"Do you miss your mother, too, young lady?"

"Yes."

"I taught my son to always share."

Halko heard his mother's words and let go of her, stepping to one side. She kept her arms open and Windy hugged her, releasing twenty-five years of tears for the mother she never knew.

"Excuse me." It was Manshin Mae channeling the personality of Hermes. "I just saw a horse twice the size of the Trojan one, made of iron and stone. It's coming this direction."

Halko seemed alarmed through his tears. "We must go."

He held his mother's hand one last time. She smiled at him. "Let us think of each other every day, without sadness."

He nodded. "Yes."

Then Manshin Mae waved her index finger as if it was a caduceus, and a cloud swirled around them and they again were aloft, Windy in the guise of the great black swan.

In what seemed to take only a moment, the snows beneath them gave way to a black river which became the Han River. They were home.

Manshin Mae collapsed after the gut and Hermes was instantly back inside the hollow head of Talos. "Sorry! I was on the other side of the world!"

Boss Kang was seated in the pilot's chair. He shook his head at what he assumed was another of his accomplice's odd exaggerations.

"You were gone for less than a minute," he said. Indeed there had been a time dilation effect: the journey to the Finnish Land of the Dead had only been a matter of seconds to anybody in Seoul. "Watch this."

He made a move with the interface, the chamber shuddered, and Hermes rushed to one of the eye portals, and looking out to see Talos raise his arm forty-five degrees and make a fist.

"Wonderful," exclaimed the god.

There was a moment of comradeship between them. "Where did you just go, really?" asked Boss Kang, deciding to take advantage of the momentary closeness.

"I wouldn't lie to you," answered Hermes. "I was in the Land of the Dead of a land I had not heard of before: Fin-land.'

The gangster's good mood was evaporating in the face of what he thought were continuous lies. Or maybe psychotic fantasies?

"What do you think you are, exactly?" he asked.

"I don't think. I know. I am Hermes the way-shower, bringer of luck, guardian at the gate, guide through the garden, friendliest to humankind, hero of the hinge—it would take half the day to recite all my epithets." This was no simple shepherd, thought the being known as Hermes, and not some belligerent hacking at other belligerents with a sharp piece of bronze. This was a denizen of a technological world of some reasonable degree of sophistication. Perhaps, he thought, a kind of genuine First Contact was possible. Mind to mind. Heart to heart.

"I am a resident of the universe next door," he continued in that hope, "who, three thousand years ago, appeared to the rustics of the peninsula of Attica, clothed in a Greek body and given voice by the Greek language, who now has appeared on the Korean peninsula clothed in a Korean body and whose tongue moves to the sounds of the Korean language. My lifespan in comparison to yours is immortal. Anything else you want to know?"

"You're a funny guy," said the mobster, not believing a word. Not *capable* of believing a word. The gulf between them might have been further than the furthest star.

There was a moment of silence during which Hermes lost his smile to disappointment. Then he laughed. "Of course! Joking. I like to hear myself talk."

If there had been a chance of genuine connection between alien and human, that moment was gone. Hermes was again playing his role. "What else can this monster do?" he asked, indicating the colossal automaton.

"Just watch," was the answer.

Folklorist Halko comforted his fiancé as she recovered from the gut. The rest of the gang stood around them, waiting for him to fulfill his promise of revealing a solution.

A loud boom thundered across the city, and the ground shook.

"Seoul doesn't have a lot of earthquakes," observed ADMIN.

Sure enough, the seismic disturbance had been caused

by Talos, who had lifted one gargantuan foot and stomped it down on the street below. Which only underlined to the members of Club H how desperate the situation was getting.

"Consider this," said the folklorist, explicating his proposal. "The breakdown of the barriers between at least two different Imaginal realms and our physical reality—the entry of archetypal figures from ancient Greece into Seoul, the sudden ease with which you are able to access the figures of Korean folklore—all constitutes a kind of chaotic state of affairs, wherein, to put it simply, the center cannot hold, because there no longer is a center."

He waited as Manshin Mae translated for the group.

"What is needed now," he continued, "is a return to order."

"A bigger god," said Hungry Gal.

"Bigger perhaps," answered the folklorist. "But certainly, one whose very identity represents *stability*."

"Like a rock," ventured Windy.

"*Exactly* like that," responded Halko. "Our current battle takes place on the field of myth and legend. I can only suggest a possible direction based on an observable and recurring theme: Prometheus was chained to a rock in the Caucasus mountains, the Olympians, of course, hail from Mount Olympus—

"Sanshin," said the mudang, without translating. "We must invoke the sanshin."

"*Which* sanshin?" asked Hungry Gal with an edge of annoyance.

"Indeed," chimed in ADMIN. "There are ten thousand mountains in Korea—"

"Which means ten thousand mountain *gods*," PJ finished the thought.

"Baekdusan," explained Mae. "The *first* mountain." The typically unflappable shamaness could not keep the trepidation from her voice. "The mountain to which the divine son of the heavenly king descended, the mountain upon which grew the sandalwood tree beneath which was conceived Dangun, the first king of Korea, the first *Korean*."

"Impossible," said Hungry Gal.

"It won't be like eating rice cakes while lying down," answered the mudang. "More like trying to contain the ocean in a bucket. Or a planet in the palm of your hand. But it can be done. Hypothetically."

"It has to be me," said Windy to Hungry Gal.

They had both waited a few moments for the others to leave the terrace—and leave the two of them alone.

"Because you're the new hotshot?"

"Because I can do it."

"So can I."

"The Haetae like me more than they like you," countered Windy.

"They told you that?"

"They don't talk."

"I know what they do and don't do."

"It was my *impression*," admitted Windy.

"Bastards. Wait till I see them again."

"You heard the manshin. Whoever does this might not survive."

"That's true for either of us."

They both thought about that for a moment.

"Maybe we should just let them fight it out," said Windy. "Until they're done."

"No way."

"It won't take much longer—"

"That's not the point," said Hungry Gal. "Think about our two lovebirds."

"Manshin Mae and Folklorist Halko?"

"Instead of them being so nauseatingly reasonable

all the time, what if they were throwing our furniture at each other or throwing each other through our walls like nobody else lived here. Would we just sit back and let them? Wait until they're done?"

"I guess not."

"We'd kick their asses out."

"She was right, of course. If the Olympians had minded their own business three thousand years ago, the worst between Troy and Greece would have been a disagreement about import duties on olive oil and feta cheese.

"That pantheon could not have cared less about the fact that they were in somebody else's world. With our own gods and monsters, our own history and traditions. Our own way of viewing the world and the world next door. It was a matter of—"

"Show some respect, you jerks."

"Exactly," confirmed Hungry Gal.

"I'll do it." "It's got to be me."

They both said it at once.

"The Club can afford to lose the new girl," said Windy of herself. "It would fall apart if they lost you."

"You said it yourself: even the Haetae don't like me."

"They *fear* you. That's a healthier dynamic for the

long term, I think." She indicated the mansion. "You keep this place together."

"ADMIN does that."

"He's more like that thing in the back of a boat," ventured Windy. "The steerer."

"The rudder?"

"And you're the big wooden part."

"The boat, basically."

"Right."

"Metaphors are not really your thing, are they?"

"Rock, Paper, Scissors."

So they did. And Windy won three times in a row.

"Again," insisted Hungry Gal.

"No."

Moments later they were headed down into the basement.

"I'm afraid," Windy said to the shamaness after catching up to her.

"So you got the job," said Manshin Mae.

"You didn't exactly step forward."

"That little Greek boy was bad enough. It's going to take me weeks to recover. I think this one... might kill me."

"And not me?"

"If you freestyle it like you people always seem to do," was the mudang's response, "then you have good reason to be afraid. Follow me. I'll dance you through the whole thing."

"How is that going to help?"

"The dancing and the music are the means of entering a receptive state of awareness, as the prelude to the invocation. But they also provide a structure that orders and protects the psyche. It keeps your mind from breaking."

"That's good to know," said Windy, not believing a word of it.

"The Haetae have paved the way through your synapses. If you can run with a herd of them, you can do this."

"I can't dance."

"That might be a problem."

Athena and Apollo had just watched with shocked surprise as Talos had stomped its foot and rattled the ground.

"The monster appears inevitable," observed Athena.

"And to think," said Apollo, "we were using it as an excuse to battle one another."

"What excuse do I need? I can take you at any moment I desire."

"Even *this* moment?" smiled Apollo. "When your great spear is in two pieces. When your aegis has exhausted its voice. When even the chest with the thunderbolts that you stole from our father—"

"Borrowed—"

"Is empty."

"Yes," Athena replied. "Even now—"

She whipped the spear tip toward his chest at impossible speed, but he blocked it with his golden bow. They both leapt backward away from each other and took a moment to assess each other's stances. Then the duel was on.

Windy was in the basement with the rest of the house, trying to follow the steps of Manshin Mae in time to her elderly musicians. As they danced, ADMIN finished lighting several torches and the flames illuminated the back walls, revealing four-thousand-year-old paintings on the stone surfaces, depicting human figures at the base of a spare triangular shape that jutted into the space above them, seemingly higher even than the sun and moon and stars rendered alongside.

Baekdusan.

"Even before there were tigers, before anybody smoked, before anything else existed, there was the mountain. It was all there was between Earth and Heaven. The biggest thing our ancestors could imagine. And I was supposed to go and get it.

Windy followed the gyrations of Manshin Mae, felt the ancient paintings move off the walls and float in midair, the mountain no longer static but animated, no longer confined to the dimensions of the ancient stone circle of the basement, but extending downwards into the core of the planet and upward into space.

She felt herself running with the Haetae across the mythical landscape of dolmen stones and winding streams of primordial water; straddling the line between our world and the one next door. She was the pack leader and viewed that world through her Haetae eyes. Then, when she felt the air stir just above her, she leapt out of the Haetae and became the swooping bonghwang, as it and she climbed into the air.

In one beat of her powerful wings, she shot north across the DMZ of the physical realm, two more beats and she could see Baekdusan itself, fully expecting to reach it in the next moment. But as she got closer, the mountain became larger, wider and taller, looming above and beyond her. The everyday world faded away and the Imaginal replaced it completely: here, Baekdusan was beyond immense, it looked to her as if it was the only thing there was, all that even could be. Higher and higher she climbed, aiming for the unseen summit that now seemed ten thousand light-years away.

And here, in the rarified upper atmosphere, her wings, or maybe it was her nerve, failed her. Windy felt herself faltering, no longer rising. Then, just as she feared she would start to fall back, she felt something else: a wind from below. She glanced down to see more bonghwang than she could count, their iridescent feathers of black, white, red, yellow, and green forming a mantle across the sky below, curving with the Earth, the beating of their innumerable wings pushing the thin aerial substrate further than what was otherwise possible, and Windy took heart and took wing, to the very edge of space.

Where she leapt from the bonghwang, climbed alone and unaided through empty ether, seeming to pass through veil after veil into increasingly larger and more subtle realms: the Imaginal beyond the Imaginal beyond the Imaginal. And each time the mountain became even bigger. And Windy wondered, recalling the old line about "it's turtles all the way down" — maybe it was also turtles all the way up. Then suddenly she had a new pair of eyes, each the size of a galaxy.

Windy had merged with the mountain, the Korean archetype of the universe itself.

Zeus suddenly felt something unexpected. An intuitive nudge of sorts, that it was time to go. "Fellas," he said. "I really must leave you. My children are missing me."

Eyepatch dismissed the idea. "You said they were inconsiderate."

"I complain too much. As we all do," replied Zeus.

"Let them wait," said Walking Stick. "You're allowed to have fun, as well. It can't just be all about the kids, all the time."

"How much longer?" asked Zeus.

"We're immortal, too," shrugged Eyepatch, with a smile.

Zeus hated abasing himself, but he was getting desperate. "If you really do think of me as a friend, then please, I ask you as a friend. Let me go."

The two across the table glanced at each other, as if duly considering their favorite new companion's words. Finally, they compromised.

"If you can throw me in a wrestling match," proposed Walking Stick, "you can do as you wish."

Zeus couldn't help but glance down: the man only had one functioning leg, after all. "What's the catch?"

"No catch," said his challenger.

"All right."

Walking Stick stood away from the table, propping himself on his cane. Eyepatch stood up as well.

And Zeus found himself in a sand-covered ssireum wrestling ring that had appeared in the middle of the small, three-way intersection in front of the CU mart. A large stack of dolmen stones was at one end of the wresting ring, the traffic light at the other. It was as if the mythological realm was superimposed over that of the everyday world of this street. None of the passersby took notice. A taxi passed right through the stones.

The dokkaebi suddenly appeared in their true forms: Eyepatch had a single eye in the middle of his forehead and stood to one side as a referee for the match. Walking

Stick had a single leg emerging downward from his torso, upon which he stood with no hint of being off-balance or otherwise compromised. Both had fierce features and extremely strong limbs, and their appearance would have terrified any mortal. Zeus, having seen pretty much every scary thing that there was to see in his corner of reality, from hundred-headed Hydra to Typhon, father of all monsters, took the goblins' appearance in stride. He was more concerned about what he couldn't see: the hidden and unexpected abilities of his opponent. He was, of course, right.

"Go!" said Eyepatch.

Before Zeus could even assume an appropriate wrestler's stance, Walking Stick bounded over with shocking speed and then hooked his single leg around Zeus' knees—and threw him to the sand.

"Win!" shouted the ref, shooting one hand sideways to signal the victory.

Zeus had no choice but to stand and face his opponent again.

"Win!"

And again.

With a sinking feeling, Zeus Lee realized this match could go on... forever.

Seated on the throne inside the head of the cloud-scraping robot, Boss Kang expressed an intent with only his mind: suddenly all the various interfaces extended from their consoles and applied themselves to his head and limbs, and he saw through the eyes of the colossus, felt his own movements reflected in its enormous body. "I'm ready," he said. "I can feel it."

"Every journey," smiled Hermes, "starts with a single step."

And on that truism, the mobster lifted his foot fifty meters into the air, and took his first step: crushing one of the abandoned dump trucks on the construction site around them, breaking clear of the fencing and what was left of the "do not trespass" tape.

Surprising even himself, Apollo had put Athena on the defensive. He was plucking the strings of his divine, tortoiseshell lyre, and the thin strands of sacred sheep gut were slashing outward from the instrument like bullwhips, crisscrossing Athena's aegis breastplate without effect, but sometimes catching her wrists and ankles and throwing her off her feet.

When Talos moved without warning, she instantly took cover behind its massive leg, avoiding Apollo's attack. When the lyre string again tried to find her, she grabbed it and wrenched hard, looping it around the automaton's ankle as it again lifted and moved forward. The lyre was jerked from Apollo's hand and Athena yanked it towards her with the loose string and flung it under Talos' sandal just as it came down; her brother's divine instrument was crushed beneath its sole.

Suddenly, a massive shadow crossed over them, the unearthly kind of penumbra that comes from an eclipse just before it hits totality.

They looked up to find the source, but could only see the bright, noonday sun and what seemed an occluding shape of unimaginable size passing in front of it. Then all was darkness.

Three times, crossing from one edge of high noon to the other, Seoul went dark as a black hole, corresponding to the shifting of the spirit of the cosmic mountain in and out of our world.

At the wrestling ring in front of the CU mart, Zeus was fed up. He had just been thrown for the hundredth time. "*Enough*," he said, as his anger at long last erupted into meteorological effect: a thunderbolt blasted the ring from above and everything went flying.

When Zeus picked himself up from the debris, he saw that his opponents had already done the same. The dokkaebi were unharmed by the worst he could do. They were, however, just a little bit sad.

"We're not angry," said Eyepatch.

"We're disappointed," agreed Walking Stick.

Then a shadow passed overhead and none of them could see a thing. A moment later, the sunlight returned.

Zeus was no longer there.

It was to be her first dive with them. They brought an extra wetsuit and hood, mask and fins, weight belt and tools for dislodging mollusks and cutting seaweed.

But just as they reached the tidepool and were about to suit her up, the sun was occluded and an immense shadow passed over where they were standing.

Aphrodite glanced down at her hands: for a moment, it seemed like she could see right through them to the sand at her feet. She glanced up and saw the expressions on the two other women's faces: they had seen it too. But at this point in the brief but eventful time she had spent with them, it was not a shock, only some kind of confirmation of what they had grown to suspect: that the young woman did not belong here.

"I think," said Aphrodite, "I have to go now."

"I'm sorry to hear that," said Haenyeo Pang. "For her sake." She moved off to let her cousin be alone with the young woman.

"I know you are not my daughter," said Haenyeo Nam quietly, embarrassed about claiming to have brought such beauty into this world.

"Child," replied the goddess, kissing her on the forehead. "You are mine." And in that instant, the grief of twenty years left Haenyeo Nam like a butterfly.

Aphrodite turned toward the sun, staring up into the fiery brightness. Yet another massive shadow crossed the solar disc and swept across the island.

After it passed, she was gone.

The Talos warrior had taken two massive steps forward, covering as many city blocks, shaking buildings and cracking the asphalt beneath its feet.

Hermes watched from behind one of the great eye openings. "Nice work. Keep going. All the way to the river." Then he noticed something above, something obscuring the disc of the sun, and his intuition told him he only had moments left to watch the apparently inevitable conclusion of his time in this realm—or to resist.

A shadow obliterated all light from the outside world, leaving the glow from the control interface as the only source of illumination.

And Hermes flew.

In the blink of an eye, he was far beyond the Earth, had seen the unfathomably huge mountain, and had felt the presence of Windy Lee. But perceived that the human essence of her was like a candle on the surface of the sun: the immensity that she had fused with was so inhuman that the young woman he had followed into this world was unreachable to him, and therefore immune to his persuasive wiles, his deceptions, his lies, or even, as a last resort, a genuine entreaty. There was no basis on which for him to communicate. He could not hope to cajole a mountain the size of the universe itself.

Still, he could fight. Did he not battle against the giants who stormed Olympus? And there were a hundred of them. This was just one... *rock*. No matter the size. He could buzz around its summit, distract it for a few moments. Until Athena and Apollo came to his side, until even Zeus joined the battle, emptying his strongbox of every thunderbolt within...

"Brother… where are you?" He heard the voice, coming from further away than he could fathom.

"Brother…" came a second voice. "Can you hear us?"

And then: "Son. We need you now."

Hermes sighed. How could he refuse?

And in another blink of an eye, he was back in the hollow head of Talos.

"What's happening out there?" asked Boss Kang, indicating the passing shadow.

"I am a purveyor of luck and a friend to the friendless, I love gambling and I'm a companion to thieves," replied Hermes. "But first and always, I am a guide for my family. And because of that role, I must say goodbye."

"What are you talking about?"

"I'm curious," asked the god. "Nobody trusts me, and with good reason. But you did. From the start. Why?"

The mobster shrugged. "You got a good face."

"Hermes of the Good Face." The god tried it out as his newest appellation. "I like it."

Then the shadow had passed, Boss Kang was standing on the ground and Hermes was nowhere to be seen. Talos towered above, but the sun seemed to be shining right through it, as if the unconquerable metal that it was composed of had become insubstantial. The gangster reached out and tapped the sandal in front of him; the behemoth came apart like spun sugar, evaporating as it fell. Nothing was left to hit the ground.

The magical device was also gone. But the backpack he had carried it in was next to him on the street, open. He looked inside: it was filled with bundles of cash. A parting gift from his collaborator, who had stolen all of it from multiple sources in the microsecond before he departed.

The Boss hoisted the backpack and decided that it was such a nice day he would walk across town to his neighborhood.

ADMIN Yoon sat in one of the library's club chairs, his bible in hand. Technically, it belonged to the Club, but since he was the only member who ever read it—and even then, infrequently—he considered it his. The pain from his "ailment of the blood" had increased by an order of magnitude over the events of the past few days; so had his desire to be released from it. And from this world.

He thought about opening the book at random and assuming that the first line he saw had been chosen for him by spiritual guidance, but wasn't that treating the Word of God as an oracle? Or even just a Magic 8 Ball? And so he opted instead to revisit a passage he knew: "Therefore I tell you, whatever you ask in prayer, believe that you have received it, and it will be yours."

Then he prayed out loud. "Lord, please let your servant Apollo change his mind."

The beings with the Korean faces who had once had Greek faces and been known as Zeus, Athena, Apollo and Aphrodite were walking across the legendary landscape of the ancient Korean peninsula, crossing a valley strewn with giant stone tables and the occasional tiny volcano. They appeared dazed and disoriented. But Hermes, their guide, walked before them and seemed to know the way, as knowing the way was his nature, though he also knew that the passage was full of perils that his family could not perceive. Not just the iron-horned lion-dogs that seemed to be stalking the Olympians, or the great, multicolored bird overhead that kept crying out unnervingly. The god of borders and liminality itself detected things only half seen, both following them, and even, at times, attempting to usurp his guidance: a bird with a human face, a horse with wings, and most elusive, a multi-tailed white fox—seven, eight, nine? It moved too quickly for Hermes to count the appendages, but he intuited that the creature was as cunning as he, and could lead them to destruction if he were not exceedingly careful.

Up ahead was a cleft in the side of the valley, and behind it could be glimpsed a much different landscape: that of the ancient Mediterranean mythological realm and of Olympus itself. It was there that Hermes Psychopomp was taking them. And as they got closer, he felt the pursuing, disrupting presences start to recede.

Hermes finally reached the chasm and passed through. After him came Zeus walking arm in arm with Aphrodite, then Athena, carrying the halves of her broken spear. Last was Apollo.

Suddenly, without seeming to think about it, the god of archery turned around and lifted his hands: his golden bow appeared, golden shaft notched and ready. He let loose the arrow.

It flew back the way they had just come, past the huge, stacked stones, until the stones became skyscrapers, continued across the great city of Seoul, unimpeded by hills or walls or glass or wood: the golden arrow went through it all, as though all was insubstantial mist. Until it passed through the parapet and panels of a hanok, and penetrated the heart of its target.

And ADMIN felt himself slip into a gentle death. He closed the bible on his lap, and never again opened his eyes.

Following behind the ancient Greek deities as they entered the Olympian realm, at a discrete distance in case anybody might object, was PJ. As he hiked along, he replayed in his mind the conversation he had had with Windy before he left her.

"I think he's still over there," PJ had said.

"Poet?"

"Who else."

"So I get to lose you too?"

"I know he hurt you. If you tell me you never want to see him again, I might reconsider going."

They had taken each other's hand.

"Come back to me," said Windy. "Both of you."

"I promise."

Then they pinky promised, stamped it with their thumbs, signed with their index fingers, and printed it with the palms of their hands so the promise could not be broken.

The erstwhile Lee family reached the rift of the valley and were hiking through it, vanishing into the other side.

PJ followed and then paused for a moment in his own

native realm for one last look, committing the megaliths to memory, in case the time should come when his current existence seemed like a daydream or a passing fantasy, and maybe the dolmens would be the only anchors to his old self, to Seoul, to the people he loved.

Then he, too, disappeared into the Olympian fastness.

And the rift itself vanished along with him, closing the door between the two worlds.

There was a wedding and a funeral.

ADMIN's ashes were laid to rest under a tree in a forest memorial park. The cremation facility had trouble lighting its furnace and the operation took several times longer than what was considered reasonable and so they charged the Club for the added time and expense. Hungry Gal had taken over ADMIN's responsibilities and she refused to pay, preferring to fight it out in court.

Manshin Mae and Folklorist Halko were married at a traditional hanok in Seoul and honeymooned on Jeju Island, where they took a ferryboat to a small picturesque island, ate oranges, took photos of the stone grandfathers and admired the haenyeo.

"And they lived happily every after. Of that, I'm pretty certain. It was a match made in Heaven, Hell, and some places in between."

Windy found the same traditional Korean oil lamp she had been introduced to during her first few days at the mansion. She lit the wick, and for once, the tiny fire didn't seem to resist coming alive in her presence.

She set it in the window.

"I hoped the flame could be seen from across the street, from across Seoul, from as far away as the stars and the next universe. A lamp that said what every lamp, placed in every window, has always said: come home."

The writer reimagines familiar Korean mythology, adding new layers to create a spectacular blockbuster with dazzling imagery. Readers will be fascinated to witness the exciting process of Haetae, a familiar figure from mythology and also a mascot, coming to life in reality.

- **Ewhan KIM**, Author

The writer demonstrates the essence of 'K-World' fiction, as showcased in the previous work "King Sejong the Great," with no less brilliance in this piece. The warp narrative in the work, which combines Korean shamanism and psychoanalytic techniques based on the mythological figure of Haetae, is remarkable. The story of Windy and the Haetae team's efforts to stop the mysterious being causing fires using shamanistic symbols is as captivating as Christopher Nolan's film "Inception," if not more so.

- **Mujin CHA**, Author

Recommendation

The novel "Haetae" is filled with vivid imagery and dynamism, akin to watching a movie. The author blends ancient Greek mythology and Korean folklore with alchemy to create a fantasy world. It's worth looking forward to the birth of a Korean version of the Marvel series. This is a glimmer of hope raised by the Star Trek writer in dark times.

- **Myung-Se LEE**, Film director

It's a delight to see a master science-fiction screenwriter turn his unique talents to mythological fantasy. This is a dazzling storytelling form that discards conventions, blending novel and screenplay to create an engaging, wild and witty fable that grips the reader from start to finish. A spectacular reimagining of a vital icon of Korean history, and a timely reminder to celebrate the past as we look to the future.

- **Daniel Martin**, Associate Professor of Film Studies, School of Digital Humanities and Computational Social Sciences, KAIST

A few years ago, when the Marvel comic "Tiger Division" was introduced to the world, I was thrilled that a Korean hero had finally emerged. To me, the novel "Haetae" carried a different significance. While a story featuring Korean cultural characters, or more precisely East Asian cultural characters, set in Korea might feel somewhat familiar, "Haetae" felt refreshingly new. Moreover, the clash between Western and Eastern mythology from the outset was thrilling.

"Haetae" is always around us, something we're bound to encounter, yet it feels like we haven't really seen it. Why haven't we appreciated its cultural value and entertainment until now? It's as if we've overlooked something precious right under our noses. As you continue reading the work, despite knowing it's fantasy, it begins to feel like the real world. The writer skillfully weaves a complex web around the protagonist, never letting the sympathy-inducing situations become stagnant. Witnessing the writer's prowess and approach, one can sense the vastness of the world within the story. Now is the time to put "Haetae" to the test on the global entertainment stage as another sensation of East Asian characters and content, to see its firepower and allure.

- **Ji-tae YOO**, Actor·Film director

The Star Trek writer has created new stories based on our mythology. The world he has crafted is so enchanting that it feels like we could just step into the pages of the story. Additionally, we are excited to see how it will be brought to life on screen.

- **Myung Seob CHUNG**, Author